A Cursed Moon

A WEIRD GIRLS NOVELLA

CECY ROBSON

Praise for A Cursed Moon

"I cannot get enough of Ms. Robson's Weird Girls. I'll say it again and again; I love her work, and this is one series I recommend to any PNR or UF readers." -
Under the Covers Book Blog

"I am usually not a fan of all the little side novellas in a series. In truth, I normally skip them. That did not stop me from scooping up, *A Cursed Moon*, and consumed it in a single sitting. I read this for the simple fact that I cannot get enough of this world and its characters...The story had suspense, danger, humor, and a few brilliant twists. Favorite characters make an appearance and enhance this story. I laughed and cried as I read this tale."   -
Caffeinated Book Reviewer

"I loved this novella! I have to admit that I am a huge fan of Cecy Robson since I read the first book in this series! Really, this woman knows how to write urban fantasy!" –
Love & Live to Read

"I adore Cecy Robson for being able to build such a fabulously complex character in a single novella...For a novella, *A Cursed Moon* is pretty eventful and it brings some permanent changes, which is rather unusual. I can't wait to see how they will reflect on the series as a whole in *Cursed by Destiny*, the next novel in this wonderful series." - **The Nocturnal Library**

"*A Cursed Moon* is a delightful, action-packed read that will keep you satisfied until you can get your hands on the next installment in the series...." - **The Book-aholic Cat**

"Cecy Robson's *A Cursed Moon* was as fantastic as all the reviews I read said it was! This short little read is an action-packed adventure and not one to be missed if you're a fan of the Weird Girls series! " - **A Great Read**

"The story in *A Cursed Moon* is action packed and go go go as it is in all of the books in this series...Seriously, if you are a fan of quick paced, action filled urban fantasy tales featuring interesting super naturals that are on an emotional yet quirky journey, then you must give this series a try. And if you are already reading it, get this novella." –
Yummy Men & Kick Ass Chicks

"This is the kind of novella I love to read. It is filled with familiar characters, there is plenty of action, some humor, and it moves the series along. Bren can be amusingly abrasive in his human form. As a werewolf, this lone wolf, is extremely dangerous...As with all of the Weird Sisters novels there is a strong ensemble of characters, the writing is enjoyable and the pacing terrific."   **- The Quillery**

"An action-packed adventure that I couldn't put down. Bren is such a great character that you really fall in love with him A great fun novella to read in the Weird Girls series." –
Books of Love

"The story, typical to Cecy Robson style is action packed…If you're a fan of Cecy Robson's Weird Girls novels this is a must read. If you haven't started this series yet. I highly recommend it!"   **- Where the Night Kind Roam**

"Oh Bren! I so love your storytelling voice *A Cursed Moon* was beyond entertaining thanks to you! *A Cursed Moon* is as fast paced, lively and dangerous as the previous books. Cecy Robson always adds these curious creatures into the mix. It'll be a long a$$ time before I get tired of the series."
- Talk Supe

"I've got to tell you, in my opinion, fans of this series MUST read this novella before the next book in the series, *Cursed by Destiny*. This isn't your ordinary "filler" novella...I could read and re-read this story over and over and over again and still smile over the silliness (and love) that is Bren."
- My Para Hangover

The Weird Girls Series

Gone Hunting
A Curse Awakened: *A Novella*
The Weird Girls: *A Novella*
Sealed with a Curse
A Cursed Embrace
Of Flame and Promise
A Cursed Moon: *A Novella*
Cursed by Destiny
A Cursed Bloodline
A Curse Unbroken
Of Flame and Light
Of Flame and Fate
Of Flame and Fury (coming soon)

The Shattered Past Series

Once Perfect
Once Loved
Once Pure

The O'Brien Family Novels
Once Kissed
Let Me
Crave Me
Feel Me
Save Me

The Carolina Beach Novels
Inseverable
Eternal
Infinite

<h1 style="text-align: center;">APPS</h1>

Find Cecy on *Hooked – Chat stories APP* writing as
Rosalina San Tiago
Coming soon: *Crazy Maple's Chapters: Interactive Stories*
APP: The Shattered Past and Weird Girls Series

The night I was born, a bat swept down in front of my father as he ran along a cobblestone road. My father ignored the bat in his haste to reach the Central American hospital where my mother labored with me. The bat disappeared in the shadows. In its place emerged a man, his dark skin bare, his voice ominous, his imposing form blocking my father's path. "Be wary of this one," he warned in Spanish. "She's not like the others."

Okay, I'll confess. This didn't happen. But it sounds way cooler than simply admitting my father used to kiss me goodnight wearing vampire fangs, and that he was the first person to trigger my overactive imagination.

I've always loved telling stories and getting a laugh. I've also enjoyed hearing stories, especially of the paranormal variety. Being of Latin descent, I heard many tales of spirits who haunt the night, of death lurking in the darkness waiting to claim her victims, and of circumstances which could only be explained by magic and creatures not of this earth.

The stories frightened me. I often slept clutching a crucifix while my plastic glow-in-the-dark Virgin Mary stood guard on my nightstand. And still I begged for more.

Sometimes the beasties of the night bumped too hard, and I swear I could see ghosts floating above me. I trekked on despite my fear, surviving each night while my plastic protector looked on.

On May 1, 2009, I decided to write a story about four unique women who must trek through their own darkness where supernasties bump hard, and bite harder. *The Weird Girls* series is the journey of Celia, Taran, Shayna, and Emme Wird, sisters who obtained their powers as a result of a backfired curse placed upon their Latina mother for marrying outside her race. Their story begins when the supernatural community of Lake Tahoe becomes aware of who they are, and what they can do.

"Weird" isn't welcomed among humans, nor is it embraced by those who hunt with fangs and claws, who cast magic in lethal blows, and who feast on others to survive. I wanted to show "weird" could be strong, brave, funny, and beautiful.

My "weird" girls will often face great terror, just like my seven-year-old frightened self, except without a glow-in-the-dark icon to keep them safe. Despite their fears, they fight like their lives depend on it, with only each other to rely on.

Sometimes, the darkness will devour the sisters. And sometimes, good won't succeed in kicking evil's ass. But just like glow-light Mary, there is hope. And there is humor—often twisted, a little inappropriate, and always hilarious—very much like a father saying goodnight to his children wearing a rubber ghoul mask and owning a collection of fake fangs no adult male should possess.

So, read on and check out my *Weird Girls* series. Maybe you'll find I'm really "not like the others."

Salud!

Cecy

ACKNOWLEDGMENTS

There are two people who I wouldn't be here without: my agent, Nicole Resciniti, and my husband, Jamie. Nicole works to make my writing dreams a reality. Jamie believed in me from the very first pages I typed. I'm so blessed to have them in my life.

Chapter One

"Damn it, Bren—wake up!"

"Hmmph?" Someone with a death wish was shaking me. You don't disturb a werewolf's sleep; that's just common fucking sense. The breeze shot through the cracked opened window, bringing a strong whiff of Tahoe's magic. I grinned and inhaled. That shit was better than witch ganja, and it lulled me back to sleep.

But then Dan flipped on the leg lamp on my nightstand and opened his yap again. "Wake up, I mean it."

"Grrrrr."

"You can take that werewolf shit and shove it up your ass."

That made me chuckle into my pillow. Dan swearing was damn funnier than Elmo dropping the "F" bomb. He shook me again, this time harder. I flipped over and tried to get comfortable.

"For crying out loud, put some pants on! I don't need to see your . . . *stuff*."

"It's my goddamn room. I can sleep naked if I want. And what the hell do you mean by 'stuff'? What are you, ten?"

Dan ignored me. "Bren, your stupid one-night stand stole all our food, our DVDs, *and* our laundry detergent."

I half-opened one eye. "Wendy wouldn't do anything like that."

"Her name was Natasha."

"You sure?"

"That's the name she wrote all over my bathroom with her lipstick."

I sat abruptly, suddenly panicked. "She didn't take my porn, did she?"

Dan's jaw slacked. "Is that all you care about, that she took your porn?"

"*No*. For shit's sake I'm hungrier than hell. How are you going to fix me breakfast without any food?"

Dan threw his hands in the air, in that same exaggerated way he always did when I pushed him to his breaking point. He kicked my dirty clothes on the floor and paced like an expectant dad. "You have the audacity to think I'd actually cook you breakfast—after what your one-nighter did?"

I scratched my beard. Damn, I needed a trim. "Well, yeah. It's your job around here, you're the woman. You're supposed to cook, clean, and pay most of the bills. My job is to keep your ass safe from humans, vamps, *weres*, witches, little old ladies, and pretty much anything else you're afraid of. It's part of our deal, along with me getting you laid."

Dan stomped to the side of my bed, stumbling over a pair of my old jeans. "First of all, it was just that one little old lady. I may be human, but I'm pretty sure she was some kind of spirit—especially given the amount of supernatural activity around here lately. Secondly, I don't need help getting laid."

I stared at my beanpole roommate. His messy curly hair hung over his thick black-framed glasses, and he tripped over air on a regular basis. *Jesus*. There were Girl Scouts more muscular and agile than him. "Yes, you do, Dan."

"I've gotten laid a lot lately, all without your help."

"Ugly girls don't count, man."

"Celia's not ugly."

I laughed and yanked at my overgrown hair. Damn, I needed a cut, too. But unlike Dan, I did grunge well. "Celia was more than eight years ago." I chuckled again. Talk about a mercy lay.

He narrowed his eyes. "What's so funny?"

"I still can't believe you were her first. How'd you talk

her into it? Did you promise to tutor her in chemistry or something?"

Dan's entire face reddened, making him look more like a tomato than a walking piece of broccoli. "Whatever, Bren. I'll prove to you I can get laid."

"Sure, sure, you can get laid. Don't get your thong in a bunch."

Dan stamped his foot. Shit, I only thought girls did that.

"I mean it, Bren. I have to work late at the lab tonight, but I'll meet you at eleven at the Watering Hole. I'm going to get a girl so hot your head will spin."

I yawned. "Sure you will, buddy."

"Fine. If you don't believe me, how about we bet on it?"

"Dan, you don't want to bet me on something like that. You'll only lose and embarrass yourself."

"You're just afraid. I thought you were a wolf, not a chicken."

My brows furrowed and I snarled. "Did you just call me a *chicken*?" This time it was Dan's turn to laugh. I could be pretty damn intimidating, but he knew I'd never hurt him. He was a mothering pain in the ass, but also the best friend I'd ever had.

"You heard me, clucky."

A slow grin eased across my face. "All right then, name the terms."

"The loser has to clean and cook for the rest of the year . . ."

"Is that the best you can come up with? Oooh, I'm real scared now."

". . . wearing a French maid's outfit, regardless of who's in the apartment."

My grin widened. The little turd had some balls after all. "You're on." I held out my hand. He refused to shake it until after I showered.

I glanced at my dogs-playing-pool clock. "Oh shit."

"What's wrong?"

"I was supposed to meet Aric and his Warriors an hour ago at the Den." I shrugged. "Oh well. They should know better than to expect me to be on time."

Dan shook his head in a way that told me a lecture was coming. "Bren, what's wrong with you? You should feel honored that Aric invited you to join his pack. He's a renowned and respected pureblood."

I kicked off the sheets wrapped around my ankles and stood, feeling my temper rise. "He only asked me to keep tabs on Celia."

Dan followed me to my closet where I yanked out my last pair of clean jeans and a flannel shirt. "He asked you because you earned his respect when you helped save her and her sisters. Bren, we would have lost Shayna if you hadn't tracked her."

I threw the clothes over my shoulder. "Whatever, he's an asshole for dumping Celia."

Dan leaned against my dresser while I reached in to grab socks and a pair of boxers. He seemed bummed all of a sudden. But hell, watching our girl Celia get chewed up and spit out had been a nut-punch none of us needed. For all her strength and good looks she'd never had any confidence when it came to males. And thanks to that idiot pureblood, she never would again.

Dan pushed his thick glasses back in place when they slid down his long schnoz. "Bren, Aric didn't have a choice. He has to marry another pureblood *were*. Even Celia has come to terms with that."

I rammed my finger in his face. "That's bullshit. You've seen her, she's not the same, and everyone damn well knows it." I stormed into the bathroom and slammed the door, cracking the doorframe. I didn't want to talk about Aric and Celia anymore. That ass-wipe broke her heart. Then he had the balls to get pissed when she turned to that master vamp prick, Misha.

I took my sweet time getting ready and then drove from Incline Village to Squaw Valley. The Den sat on top of Granite Chief Peak, not exactly the best terrain for my '71 Mustang, but screw it. I wasn't giving up my wheels just because I signed up to teach a bunch of snot-nosed little punks.

The 'stang roared up the dirt path, kicking up pebbles every time I hit the gas. I'd like to say my baby raced up the steep incline like cougar in heat. I'd also like to say I banged Ali

Landry. Neither was true. I fought to keep my ride from swerving off the goddamn cliffs. The trek up the mountain took me fifteen hellish minutes. Talk about a pain-in-the-ass commute.

Waves of magic thickened the closer I got to the entrance. The *weres* and the local coven of witches had combined their mojo to reinforce protective wards surrounding the mountain and any place used as a safe house for preternaturals. Dan was right about one thing; spooks had been popping up around Tahoe like gophers . . . gophers who liked eating people. It wasn't exactly a shock. Since the Tribe had emerged a lot of mystical shit had gone down. And since our recent run-in with the demon lords leading them, the amount of spirits lurking about had gone haywire. It hadn't grown too bad too handle—just a couple of ghosts here and there trying to claim lives—but *hell* it was enough to keep us on our toes.

I pulled up to the iron gates. A werewolf named Bob barreled out of the gatehouse crankier than sin and roughly the age of stone. His scowl revealed his pleasure at my arrival. I flipped him off. I wasn't pleased either, pal. My hopes were that that hot blonde, Heidi, was working so I could talk her into a nooner. So much for that.

Bob growled hard enough to quiver his lips like a bulldog. Impressive—*if* I were a toddler and afraid of idiots. I blew him a kiss and peeled rubber through the gates, away from the dense forest and onto the Den's large campus. The place looked like a ritzy ski resort for those born with silver spoons rammed up their asses—not a school for teaching those who could *change* into snarling beasts at will. Giant chalets with wraparound stone-stacked porches and outdoor fireplaces made up the buildings on either side of me. I huffed. There was money in being *were*. Too bad those bastards weren't willing to share with a mutt like me.

I passed the library lawn where Koda and Liam—two of Aric's other Warriors—engaged in some kind of training activity with the young *weres*. They scowled at me. I smiled and gave them a wave. Hey, what could I say? I was a hell of a guy.

I peeled to a stop and parked in front of the administration building, a chalet that ran up three damn stories.

Aric's quarters were supposedly on the top floor. I wondered briefly if he could see God from there.

Gemini lolled down the stone steps as I slipped out of the 'stang. Out of all of Aric's Warriors, he was the most tolerant of me. It must be because of that whole Zen thing he had going on. At first I didn't understand how he and Celia's sister Taran had gotten together. She was a sexy siren and louder than a bunch of frat boys at a strip club. If he was any calmer, he'd slip into a coma. Then I saw how his laid-back nature affected her and I got it. She was his yin, he was her yang.

He probably also likes what she does to his yang. I know what I'd like Heidi to do with my . . . Shit. I wonder if I could track her.

Gemini squared his jaw, darkened by a well-groomed goatee—kind of prissy if you asked me. "Bren, Aric and I would like a word with you."

I shrugged, knowing he was pissed and knowing I could give a rat's ass. He led me across the street into the main building used for classes, recreation, and dining hall. Ten-thousand square feet of wall-to-wall dark wood awaited me down the corridor. Too bad Gemini turned left toward Aric's office.

We found Mr. Royal Among *Weres* sitting behind a mahogany desk in an office roughly the size of my apartment. He flicked a pen across a paper he was grading, kind of an odd task for a guy who's supposed to be a big shot. He angled his chin up as soon as he caught my scent and—surprise, surprise— he didn't appear happy. "Have a seat," he said through gritted teeth.

Gemini positioned himself at his right side, just like a good ole Beta should. I sat down and put my feet up on his pristine desk. *Hell, I'm already in trouble. Might as well have some fun—* I hadn't finished my thought before Aric backhanded my feet off so hard that I spun in my chair. "What the hell, Aric? Do you have your period or something?"

"Bren, when I invited you to join our pack I thought you understood it wasn't in name only. Belonging requires not only for you to fight evil alongside us, but discipline and commitment to learning our ways and educating the minds of our young males. You've been a *lone* wolf all your life, so I've let some things slide—"

"Is this about the sex-ed talk I gave the students?"

Aric gripped the sides of his desk. Any minute, he was going to smash that fine piece of furniture into rubble. I didn't care; it wasn't coming out of my paycheck. He let out a deep breath. "That wasn't a sex-ed talk," he snapped. "That was a how-to-get-laid speech."

I shrugged. "Same difference."

"No, it's not. Especially when you were supposed to be lecturing on driver's ed."

"I mentioned the driving, but that bored the shit out of them. So I talked to them about what to do in the backseat. *Believe me,* that kept their interest. I was just getting to the extra-credit assignment when you barged in."

Gemini interrupted, probably to give Aric a moment to calm down. "Bren, we keep males and females separated during their schooling in order to keep them focused on their learning and decrease their naturally competitive natures. In their teens, they're extremely impressionable and hormonal."

"You mean horny? It's okay, Gemini, you can say it. We're all adults here."

Aric leaned back in his leather chair and narrowed his stare. "Look, Bren. It's not just about the damn speech. As *weres* we're the ones obligated to protect the earth. Our war against the Tribe has reduced our numbers to a handful of scattered packs." He swore when I rolled my eyes. "Are you that blind to what's happening? It's bad enough we have demon lords to deal with, but this ghost activity is getting a hell of a lot worse!"

Shit, the guy's testy. "Don't you think I know all this?"

"Then you need to start getting here on time, start learning everything you can to make yourself a better Warrior, and assist our youth in becoming the best they can be." The knuckles in his hand cracked when he balled them into fists. He must not have liked me picking that piece of lint off my shirt just then. He growled, further emphasizing his annoyance. "*Bren,* the Elders don't approve of your presence. I'm sticking my neck out for you and I expect you to start making an effort!"

"I resent that. I make an effort. Who the hell was

pummeling evil back to hell with you just the other week?"

Aric leaned forward. "Engaging in the occasional clash with the dark ones isn't enough. You need to sharpen your fighting skills as a wolf and a human. They're average at best, and we don't know what shit we're going to face." He watched me carefully, trying to gauge my reaction to his tirade. "I can't drive this into your thick skull enough. You have to be ready and capable to take on any opponent—whether it's another preternatural or something that rises from the demon realm."

I tucked my hands behind my head, seriously not giving a crap. "Aric, you saw me in action last week. My fighting skills are awesome."

"No, they're not. You're a brawler. All those kung-fu movies you claimed to have watched are not enough. You need to study actual technique and form. It's the only way to ensure your survival and that of the earth's."

I'd survived a hell of a lot more than this rich boy and his buddies ever had. The prick was totally asking for it. "I don't have to do jack. I can kick any one of your Warriors' asses."

Aric's lips curved into a smile. "Really? You're saying you can take Gemini, Koda, or Liam?"

I leaned forward and grinned back. "Not only them, but you too, pretty boy. Any time, any place."

Aric stood slowly and walked around the desk. "How about outside, right now?"

I stood to face him and waved an arm out. "After you, sunshine."

Gemini straightened. "Bren, I don't think you realize what you're getting yourself into."

I followed Aric out, ignoring Gemini and ready to rumble.

We passed Liam and Koda leading their group inside for chow time. Liam's eyes cut to Aric then me. "What's going on?"

I puffed out my chest and winked. "Nothing, buddy. I'm just about to pound the shit out of your fearless Leader."

There was a brief pause before the tap of fingers drummed across cell phones and the stupefied group clamored behind us and hurried to catch up. By the time we crossed the street and onto the large lawn in front of the library, *weres* were rushing out of buildings and sprinting down the sidewalks from every direction. Students and faculty alike circled around us. It was about forty degrees outside, and the cloudy, overcast sky had already begun to drop the first traces of sleet. Aric yanked off his navy University of Colorado sweatshirt and tossed it aside, leaving him only in a black T-shirt. "Okay, the first guy to get pinned loses. Let's cut to the rules—"

I stripped out of my flannel shirt and tensed my muscles so they bulged. "How 'bout we chuck the rules and say anything goes?" A loud murmur spread around the crowd. "And how about the first one who gets knocked out loses?" Murmurs morphed into excited shouts. Aric just stood grinning like an idiot. Dumb shit didn't know what he was in for.

"Fine, Bren, we'll play it your way. Just to make it interesting, the loser—that would be you—has to do anything the winner—*me*—wants. Are we clear?"

"Damn straight. Ready when you are, hero."

Aric advanced. "Take your best shot."

"How about my best kick?" I led with my foot to the outside of Aric's knee. As he sidestepped away from my fake kick, I caught him with a left cross to the nose. He winced. I winked.

"Damn shame you punch like a girl." He landed a spinning heel kick to the side of my forehead when I lurched forward.

I staggered back and grunted. "Lucky kick, *asshole*."

We circled each other with our eyes locked, looking for an opening to attack. Around us the young wolves chanted, "*fight, fight, fight, fight,*" reminding me of the good ole days on the playground.

Aric attacked first with a jab. I blocked it but couldn't stop his knee from jamming into my ribs or his elbow that slammed into my chin. I went down. Aric followed, but I surprised him with my speed, meeting his jaw with a right cross.

"Oh. I'm sorry, sweet cheeks. Did that hurt?"

Aric responded with a spinning back kick into my solar plexus. I stepped back to catch my breath, but Jet Li continued with a spinning back fist into my temple and followed with a hammer fist to my forehead. For a moment, I thought my brain had actually fallen out of my skull. I shook my head to try to clear it.

Okay . . . that got my attention. When brawn failed, it paid to rely on strategy. *Time to get a little dirty.* "So, Aric, have you talked to Celia lately?"

A united gasp spread throughout the crowd, followed by a deafening silence. Even the damn birds in the trees stopped chirping.

Aric paused, shooting me a death glare hot enough to singe.

Liam cut through the mob of students. "Bren, I wouldn't mention her name if I were you."

Koda clasped Liam's arm and pulled him back to the edge of the circle. "Let him talk, Liam. We'll see just how far his mouth gets him."

My head jerked around, like I had no clue whom Liam meant. "Mention whose name? Oh! Do you mean Celia, his ex-girlfriend who's now shacking up with a *vampire*?"

Aric's deep growl rumbled low into his chest. "I'm warning you, Bren, don't go there. She's not here to save your pathetic ass."

Heh, heh, heh. Am I getting to you, lover boy? "Oh, I know she's not here, Aric. She's busy with Misha."

Aric attempted an uppercut to my chin, but his fury made him sloppy and I drove my knee into his balls. He dropped like a chunk of granite. Heh, heh . . . a snarling chunk of granite.

I stood over him and shook my head. "Sorry, Celia. . . . Well, then again it shouldn't matter to her, now that she's got Misha to help her out in that department—"

"Oh!" The crowd yelled when Aric leaped up and nailed me in the face. Two of my teeth hit the grass like hail. I kicked his boys again—more out of instinct than tactic. He hunched over in agony. I spit out a lot of blood and about three more teeth. *No worries, they'll grow back in a few hours.*

Things were starting to go my way, so I decided to have a little more fun. "You probably heard that Celia is staying in Misha's guesthouse. I heard the same thing, but I don't believe it for a minute. If I know my boy Misha, Celia is probably with him right now—if you know what I mean."

Aric broke my nose with his fist then under-hooked my left shoulder and slammed me into the frozen ground. I choked, trying to breathe, and spit out more blood.

Okay, now I'm pissed. I'd bled enough, now it was his turn. I staggered to my feet. "Nice one, Aric. Do you think that's how Misha throws Celia on the bed every night?"

My trash talk didn't have the effect I wanted. When I charged, he flipped me onto the ground again. I whirled back to my feet—not wanting him to realize how he'd knocked the wind out of me. We faced each other again, circling with challenging stares.

Enough is enough. Time for you to go down, you cocky son of a bitch. I prepared to take him out with my best move, but not before letting one last comment sink in. "So, do you think Celia screams out Misha's name? You know, when they're doing it like monkeys?"

I'm not sure how it happened exactly, but the world went black. When I opened my eyes, a hell of a long time later, it was white and I couldn't see a goddamn thing. It took me a moment to realize that it was because I had a note conveniently stapled to my forehead. It read:

Dear Loser,

From now on, you will be at the Den on time and ready to work. When you are here you will be respectful to my Warriors and to me, and you will abide by our ways. You will also be in charge of cleaning this bathroom you're lying in by six o'clock every night for the next month.

One more thing. Celia is my mate. If you ever disrespect her again, I'll tear out your fucking throat.

Sincerely,

Aric Connor

aka Your Fearless Leader, who knocked the shit out of you

I looked around. The place was an endless room of black tile and chrome. It had seven stalls, seven separate urinals, and four showers. I swore up and down. *When the hell am I going to learn to keep my mouth shut?*

I may have been an asshole, but I was an asshole who

kept his word. It took me hours to clean the damn place. *Didn't anybody teach these little pukes how to aim?* I was finishing up scrubbing the last urinal when a stampede echoed down the long corridor outside the bathroom. A pack of young wolves stormed in, occupying every last stall and urinal. Apparently, they'd just finished dinner, and judging by the sounds and smell, chili had been on the menu.

Liam, Koda, and Gemini roared with laughter outside the door as I let loose on the evil little bastards. "Hey! You better get your assess back in there and flush, you pricks. . . . *You*, aim for the hole, aim for the hole, don't look at me—*aim for the goddamn hole*! Oh, I know you assholes aren't showering now. Everyone get the hell out. . . . I don't give a shit if you're not done, get the fuck out now!"

Every last turd scrambled out leaving wads of toilet paper and dirty towels scattered across the muddy floor. I swore when I glanced at the wall clock and saw it was five-goddamn-thirty. Somehow, I was going to get the Warriors back for this.

Chapter Two

Three rolls of paper towels, a nasty scouring pad that needed to be lit on fire, and one destroyed mop later, and my ass was finally done cleaning. I barreled down the steps and almost crashed into Celia's younger sister, Emme.

Her eyes practically shot back into her skull and she clasped her hands over her mouth when she saw me. I didn't have a clue what freaked her out until I remembered my teeth hadn't finished growing back in. I greeted her with a nod of my chin and flashed her a hillbilly grin. "Wassup, Emme?"

Emme reached to touch my hand from where I stood and led me down the steps like someone's grandpa. "Oh, Bren. What happened?" She wrinkled that cute little nose of hers with all the menace of a Golden Retriever pup. "Tell me who did this to you."

"I got into a fight with another wolf. No big deal."

Her jaw popped opened. "Bren, it is a big deal. No one has a right to treat you this way. You should tell Aric right away so this lunatic doesn't get away it!"

I stopped grinning. "Ah, Emme, that's not going to happen."

"*Why?*"

"Because the lunatic was actually Aric," I grumbled.

Emme released my hands, the rising heat of her body flushing her fair skin pink. "Bren . . . what did you do to make him so mad?"

How come everyone always assumes it's my fault?

Emme didn't wait for me to answer and led me down the long stretch of hall and into the kitchen. Someone must've been on galley duty, 'cause the stainless steel appliances and granite countertops shone to spotless perfection. Unlike the bathroom upstairs.

Emme pulled out a chair and motioned for me to sit. She searched through the drawers until she found two kitchen towels. "Bren . . . Aric hasn't been in pleasant spirits these past few months."

"No shit."

She smiled softly despite not being one to swear and ran water under a towel at the sink. "I don't think you understand. What Celia and Aric shared was beautiful and rare, and something few get to experience." She squeezed out the excess water before returning to where I waited at the table. With a sigh, she gently slid the towel along my face, paying close attention to the area around my mouth and nose. "Don't be too hard on Aric. And please try to be a little more patient with him. He's hurting. In some ways, I think he hurts more than Celia."

I scoffed. "That's a hell of thing to say, seeing how he dumped your sister, knowing how much she loved him."

She stopped wiping and pulled back her hand, showing me the amount of dry blood she'd cleaned, with sadness dimming her gentle green eyes. "I'll be honest. I don't understand a lot about matehood. But I believe the wolves when they say it's what bonds my sister and Aric. I saw how Celia and he were when they were together, and I see how they are now." She offered me the dry towel. "They're miserable, Bren. They are. And I'm convinced they'll never know happiness apart."

"Which makes Aric more of an ass-hat for ending their relationship."

"Aric walked away, that's true. But I think because of it, he has more of a cross to bear." Emme played with her hands, appearing to think things through. "He knows he did this to them. The guilt alone is punishment enough, don't you think?"

"Nope."

Emme shook her head and a laugh like tinkling bells

escaped her lips. "Oh, Bren, what will I ever do with you?"

I waggled my shaggy brows at her. "Well, I do have a few minutes."

The blush returned to her cheeks and she lowered her gaze. "Liam is waiting for me upstairs. Let me help you heal before I leave." Emme's delicate fingers touched my face. I'd watched her tend to others before with her gift, but I'd never experienced her *touch* first hand. A gentle yellow light streamed from her fingertips, surrounding us both. It felt . . . nice . . . really nice, even when my jaw cracked as my new teeth found their home.

She drew her hands back slowly and angled her chin to assess her work. Damn, she was pretty, soft blond waves falling just past her shoulders and a splash of freckles across her nose. "Better?" she asked.

"Ah, yeah, Em . . . that was. . . . Thanks, just thanks." What the hell was wrong with me? Talk much, asshole?

"You're very welcome." She looked up at the kitchen wall clock. "I'd better find Liam. If I'm even five minutes late he convinces himself that some evil monster ate me." She embraced my neck, surprising me by not letting go right away and speaking with a voice heavy with sadness. "You know what I said about Celia and Aric's love being rare and beautiful?"

"Yeah?"

"As much as it hurt them, every last smile, touch, and soft word was cherished. And I bet both would give anything to experience it again." She sighed softly. "I wish Liam could love me that deeply." She released me then, and slowly my arms slipped from her back. With a small wave, and an even smaller smile, she left kitchen.

For some strange-ass reason, I was really hating Liam then.

On my way out of the building, I spotted a tall, leggy blonde carrying a couple of bags of takeout. She dressed like a slutty heiress—tight skirt hiked up high enough to crush her ovaries and a pink silk blouse skimpy enough to strain against her braless hooters. I recognized her as Aric's fiancée. She'd shown up uninvited to Shayna and Koda's wedding a few weeks ago and had caught Aric and Celia making out like a bunch of horny teens on the dance floor. She stopped short when she saw me and narrowed her amber eyes. "You're that idiot, Brian, right? Celia Weird's friend?"

A slow, easy grin inched across my face. *Sister, you just messed with the wrong wolf.* "The name's Bren. But you're right; I am friends with Celia *Wird*. You're Charlotte, aren't you?"

"My name is Barbara."

I grimaced, feigning embarrassment. "Sorry, didn't know. Aric never mentions you."

Hey, Aric said I had to be respectful of him and his Warriors. He never mentioned being nice to this bitch.

A scowl creased her face, revealing that ugly side the prima donna likely worked to keep hidden. She composed herself and licked her bright red lips. "I was just coming in to see *my fiancé*." She lifted the bags and shook them in my face. "I brought him dinner from Stan's Bar-B-Q."

I laughed.

She dropped her hands, shuffling the contents of Aric's dinner. "What's so funny?"

"You don't cook, do you?"

She lifted her chin. "So, what?"

"So? Sweetheart, there's two ways to snag a wolf—in the kitchen and in the bedroom. Celia managed both. She'd fix Aric meals like filet mignon stuffed with shrimp, and pineapple upside-down cheesecake." I shrugged. "But I guess he needed the calories since he'd rush them to bed the moment he licked that last bit of whipped cream off her lips."

Whatever restraint she had cracked like a strike of lightning. She punched me hard across the face, jolting the new teeth Emme helped me grow in. I flexed my jaw and loomed over her. Unless she went for the kill, there's no way I'd hit her back. I didn't hit girls. Period. So instead I reeled my animal side in and leaned back on my heels, smiling wider. "Bottom line, I've *never* scented you on Aric. So you can't cook." I held out a finger. "And he obviously hasn't rushed you to bed." I added another finger and wiggled them at her. "Two strikes. You're out, babe."

For several seconds all we did was breathe. She eyed my throat like she wanted a bite until she finally squared her shoulders and met my glare in challenge. "None of that matters, you ball-less little bastard. That tramp friend of yours is despised by our kind and long gone from Aric's life. I'll be his wife soon, and there's not a goddamn thing you or she can do about it." She circled me, paying close attention to the bloodstains on my flannel shirt and the rip in my jeans. "I'll have a lifetime to learn how to cook for him and pleasure him in ways that bitch never could." She whispered the last part in a low, satisfied voice. She thought she'd shut me up.

She thought wrong.

I shook my head. "Oh, I doubt you could achieve in a lifetime what Celia did for Aric in just a few months. The way I hear it, they were always at it like wererabbits."

Her skin flushed, from the crease between her puny chest up to her face. But then she took a breath and surprised me by calming,—odd, considering she wanted to munch on my jugular seconds before. *Hmm, I guess I have to work a little harder*.

"Aric has taken a vow of celibacy until we're married, out of respect for me and our relationship," she hissed. "Whatever disgusting whores he took before we met don't matter. *I'm* his mate."

I chuckled and scratched my beard. "You don't get it, do you? Aric won't touch you because you're not who he wants. This celibacy bullshit is just an excuse not to be with you until he absolutely has to. As far as Celia's concerned, she's not disgusting, she's not a whore, but she is Aric's mate."

This made her laugh pretty damn hard. She threw back her head and tossed back her long blond hair. "Really? And where did you get that asinine idea, moron?"

"Well . . ."—I reached in my back pocket and pulled out Aric's note—"it says so right here," I answered, pointing.

I jumped in my Mustang and texted Celia, telling her to meet me at her old house in Dollar Point. I couldn't watch Dan embarrass himself that night on my own. My boy needed an audience—and a witness to prove he couldn't get laid without me. I then hauled ass out of the Den, having had enough fun for the day. I munched on the food Charlotte brought for Aric on my way. She threw it in my face right before storming off to find him. As far as I was concerned, that was the same thing as telling me it was mine. It was good barbeque. Aric would have liked it.

I chuckled to myself as I remembered her screams and growls blasting down the hall when she found him. The little missus was obviously not pleased.

My Mustang roared into my girl's small cul-de-sac like a lion on the prowl, kicking up the dry leaves the chilly fall breeze had spilled into the street and making them swirl in my headlights. A silver Lexus LFA hugged the curb. I huffed and rolled my eyes, guessing that must've been Celia's assigned vamp-mobile. The vamps sucked serious ass. I wasn't cool with how Misha was trying to win her over. At least I knew Celia couldn't be bought.

Celia hadn't replied to my text telling her to meet me here. But her presence told me she'd received it. Strange, though, unless she was busy disemboweling some wicked bastard, she usually texted right back.

I jumped out and ambled toward the blue Colonial. Mrs. Mancuso, the girls' elderly neighbor, was sweeping her front steps by the light of her lawn jockey's lantern, a freak-ass little statue with bright red pants and a lazy eye. Despite the late hour she brushed her little broom back and forth with quick precise motions, even though any sap could have eaten off of the wooden steps as they were. She was probably bored, and lonely. The Wird sisters seemed to be her only form of entertainment.

She buttoned the top of her coat to protect her frail body against the cold. As a *were*, I'd keep the majority of my strength and reflexes till my dying day. Little old humans like her didn't have that luxury. I grinned with my new set of chompers and winked her way. "Hey, sex-uh lady."

Mrs. Mancuso smiled and tucked her neck skin into her brown wool scarf. "Oh, Brendan, you're such a good boy to flirt with an old lady." She furrowed her penciled in brows and glanced over at Celia's former home sweet home. "Too good a boy in fact to be hanging out with those Wird girls."

I nodded in agreement. "Don't worry, Mrs. M, I'm trying to help them see the light. I plan to spend the next few hours reading to them from the Bible. They'll come around, just leave it to me."

The front door of the Wird house crashed open. There stood Celia—five-foot-three inches of long lethal muscles in skinny jeans and a tight white long sleeved T-shirt. The breeze picked up, sweeping her long mane of brown curls around her face. She pushed her hair out of the way, exposing her narrowing green eyes. Her supersized hearing had obviously picked up my chat with her not-so-favorite neighbor.

I waved. "Hey, Ceel. What's wrong? Still mad I made you cancel your porn subscription?"

It was really hard not to laugh at her reaction. Celia subscribing to porn was like me joining a Justin Bieber fan club—so *not* happening. Her eyes shot open only to narrow further at Mrs. Mancuso's stiff, reprimanding middle finger.

Celia stormed to the edge of her front porch, and while a wide driveway separated both houses, I still caught her golden skin reddening beneath the whitening glare of her porch light. "Mrs. Mancuso, I do not have a porn—"

"Harlot!" Mrs. Mancuso shot back. She lifted her broom defensively, daring Celia to cross the driveway and step foot on her property. Celia pinched the bridge of her nose. In a Mancuso / Celia Wird smack-down, Mrs. M won every time. Not that Celia couldn't crush her like a fistful of berries, but because Ceel didn't pick on those weaker than her, no matter how much they annoyed her.

I placed my hand on Mrs. M's shoulder. "It's okay, honey-bunches. I won't stop until the sin is washed from her wanton soul."

"Bren, that's enough out of you."

Mrs. M patted my arm, ignoring Celia. "You're a good boy, Brendan," she said once more.

She flipped Celia off again before shuffling into her house. I chuckled and jogged up Celia's light blue porch steps. I topped the charts around six-five, so even one step below her I still towered over her petite form. I pinched her cheek. "What's the matter, baby girl, can't you take a joke—"

My voice cut off in a gurgled choke. Celia snatched my throat with her hand and dragged my ass into her old pad. She kicked the door shut behind us without losing her stride. Like I said, long lethal muscles. My hulking body slid across the dark wood floors. I grabbed her wrist to break her hold but from one strangled gasp to the next, she flung open the sliding glass door leading out and tossed me over her deck.

I rolled roughly twenty feet across the leaf-strewn back lawn, shocked stupid by her over-reaction. What the hell? This wasn't the first time I'd busted on her with Mancuso.

Celia scanned the darkness in a glance, searching for a goddamn witness to my execution, I assumed, before she leaped over her porch and landed in a crouch in front of me.

I scrambled to my feet. "Ceel, what the fu—"

Apparently, my BFF wasn't done. She clenched my arm and *shifted* me into the frozen ground. My body burst into a gazillion molecules, small enough to pass me through the earth like sand through a colander. I jerked, struggling to break free except all I managed to wiggle was my damn head. It was no use, her weird mojo had buried me from the neck down. I groaned. "Come on, Celia. You know I was only messing with you."

Celia stalked around my head as if debating whether to kick it out into the forest behind me. "Were you messing with me when you embarrassed me in front of Aric and his entire pack?"

My jaw popped open but I quickly shut it. I should've known. The goddamn Warriors had either ratted me out to Celia's sisters or phoned her themselves. That's when I knew it was time call in a favor to my buddy the wereskunk. The Warriors were in for a big surprise next time they climbed into their vehicles.

"Sorry, hot-stuff," I muttered.

She rounded on me. "Sorry that I found out, or sorry for acting like a monstrous prick?"

Was that a trick question? I shrugged . . . well, I tried to anyway. "Both, I guess."

"You guess? That's seriously all you have to say to me?"

"Come on, Ceel. I said I was sorry. Aren't you done yet?"

"No, I'm not done! I can't believe you would talk about me in such a repulsive way to Aric *and* his entire gang of midnight streakers! You're supposed to be my friend!"

"For hell's sake, you know I didn't mean a damn word

of it. I only meant to distract him so I'd win the fight."

"Couldn't you have distracted him another way?" Celia bent and slapped me upside the head. "Did you have to say that Misha and I do it like orangutans?"

"*I would never say that* . . . I said you did it like monkeys."

That earned me the ultimate glare. Beneath the rising moon, Celia's green eyes morphed into that of her beast and fired with anger. Her fangs had also begun to protrude, a neat trick and not something *weres* could do unless they were trying to *turn* someone into a werebeast. Her body's reaction told me two things: One, her inner golden tigress was itchin' to unleash and beat my ass. And two, shut the hell up, jackass.

"Whatever, Bren," she hissed. "Trying to win a fight at my expense is dirty and unfair. I would never do that to you!"

"Celia, everyone there knew I did it just to bust his balls. Besides, that asshole deserves a few jabs to his ego for dumping you."

I should've stuck to the "shut the hell up, jackass" game plan. Celia stilled, her eyes resuming their round human shape and her fangs dissolving back to into average incisors. She stared hard at her worn shearling boots. *Shit. Way to go, idiot.*

"What happened between Aric and me is no one else's business—do you understand me? Save your lewd comments for your drinking buddies and watch your mouth when it comes to me and him." She veered around slowly and headed toward her deck, her hips swinging in that catwalk of hers . . . though I didn't miss how her shoulders slumped slightly. Misery had that effect.

"Where you goin', Ceel?"

Celia didn't bother looking back. "To Misha's. The vamps aren't perfect, but at least when they insult me, they do it to my face. I may or may not be back to free you tonight. Enjoy the view of the backyard."

"Aric referred to you as his mate," I said quickly before she could bounce up the steps.

My comment froze her in her tracks. When she glanced over her shoulder, I thought for sure she'd let loose the waterworks. Had I been free, I would have kicked my own ass.

Her eyes brimmed with tears. "Don't you dare play with my feelings like that."

I swore a few times in my head. "Ceel, I may be an asshole. But you know I'd never intentionally hurt you. Look, get me out and I'll prove it to you."

She crossed her arms over her perky bosom. "Bren, I swear, if this a trick—"

"It's not. Come on, get me out. It's cold down here."

Celia yanked me by my moppy hair and *shifted* me free from my earth-packed prison. She waited with clenched fists ready to pound. Before I got knocked out for the second time that day, I fumbled for the note in my back pocket. She frowned when I grabbed her hand and placed the wrinkled and torn pieces in her palm.

I grinned. "Think of it as a puzzle you have to put together."

She clasped her hand over the ripped bits of paper when the wind picked up, and walked up the wooden steps leading to her deck. I followed, watching as she used a few pebbles gathered in an old mason jar to weigh down the rumpled pieces while she arranged them on her patio table. It didn't take her long to put the note back together. Debbie, or whatever the hell her name was, hadn't taken the time to shred the evidence. After all, she had an unsuspecting fiancé to deal with and the rage of a jilted werebitch to unleash.

Celia crossed her arms again and read Aric's words in silence, paying close attention to where her wolf openly proclaimed their matehood. Damn shame he never told her himself.

"Do you mind if I keep it?" she asked after a while.

I shrugged with one shoulder. "Go ahead. I think I've worn out its usefulness." I paused, wrestling with whether I should open my yap again. Aric had majorly f'd up when it came to my girl, and shattered what little confidence their relationship had brought her. It was his fault. All of it. But she needed validation that what they had had been real—and not some game he'd played to get in her pants.

She angled her chin in my direction. "What is it?"

I plucked another pebble from the mason jar and tossed

it in my hand a few times, struggling with whether to shut my trap or squeal like a little bee-otch. In the end, my loud mouth won. Hell, it usually did. "I hate to admit it, but that wolf does love you. I know I've told you before, but you need to believe it, kid."

I wandered to the edge of the deck, unable to bear her reaction. As it was, that bittersweet scent of her sadness belted my schnoz like a sucker punch. I pitched the pebble past where her property ended, swearing beneath my breath. The small round pebble soared over the cluster of bulky pines, up the steep incline, and into the forest. I heard it land a few seconds later, its dive to the ground muffled by the thick bed of pine needles carpeting the forest floor.

Celia leaned against the weathered rail next to me, her voice strained. "Maybe he does, but he'll be married soon—and it won't be to me."

I wrapped my arm around her shoulders and pulled her close. She leaned against me, despite how muddy the *shift* had left me. Celia was always cool about forgiving me. Maybe she realized I wasn't such an ass-wipe after all . . . and that I'd do anything for her and her sisters. "Come out with me tonight. You could use a good laugh."

She lifted her head. "Are you going to a comedy club or something?"

"Not exactly." I chuckled again. "Dan's convinced he can get laid without me. I'm betting he can't."

She rubbed her brow. "Oh, no. Poor Danny. For the love of all things holy, what did you bet him?"

"I—" An unearthly cold hit my spine like a frozen spike and my head whipped in the direction of the forest. The sour stench of rot and torture burned through my nose and rolled my stomach. I snarled and shoved Celia behind me. There, at the edge of her lawn, inched a spirit dressed in a sheer flowing gown of red.

Her long black hair drifted around her like bands of seaweed in water. Her coal black eyes sparkled despite the lack of moonlight where she watched us. She smiled with jagged teeth. "Have you seen my children?" she asked in an eerie cry that seemed to echo from all directions.

"Holy *shit*."
It was my only response before I attacked.

Chapter Three

"Bren, *don't!*"

I ignored Celia and leapt off the deck, landing in my six-hundred-pound timber wolf form. The spirit's high-pitched cackle raised the brown fur on my back in perfect "come and get me" mode. She disappeared through the evergreens just as my jaws opened to bite.

Normally my fangs wouldn't have done jack shit against a spirit, but this one had taken a physical form. Good for me, bad—*seriously bad*—for her. Her long sheer gown swirled like flickering flames behind her as she sprinted around the firs in a dizzying blur. Damn it, she was fast. I hauled serious tail to keep up, using the blood red color of her gown to lure me to her like a goddamn bull.

"Where are my children . . . help me find my children."

Her shrill voice mocked and taunted me, disorienting my senses as it echoed from all directions. So I ignored everything but my sight and used my speed to propel me closer to her evil, decaying ass.

My paws thundered over the thick vegetation and masses of crumbling bark. We'd barreled halfway up the mountain when I pounced. The force of my weight slammed her thin figure across the earth, digging a small trench into the soil. My claws held her down while I dug my fangs through her skull. Gray matter spilled like chunks of rotten cauliflower. She screamed with rage and pain. I had her. I totally had her.

Too bad that's when her children decided to show up.

And let me tell you, they were ugly little bastards.

Two boys donning rags of slithering insects broke through the trees and thick ferns. Their clawed little fingers stretched out, batting the air as they hissed with long, black tongues. Their eyeless sockets fixed on me. *"Mama. Mama,"* they blubbered in low, throaty voices to the beat of "red rum."

They launched onto my back, biting with sharp little teeth and puncturing their nails through my fur. I bucked and rolled, trying to hang tight to their mom and wrench the creepy shits off me. I would've managed if not for the scorching hot pain that shot through my rear. Something ripped through the muscle of my hind leg. And it wasn't pretty. It seriously wasn't pretty.

A little spirit girl about five or six, with—no lie—long writhing centipedes for pigtails, munched on my leg like it was a box of *Cracker Jacks*. Blood poured out of me like a leaky dam, splattering her dress of beetles and roaches, and making her chew that much faster.

Son of a bitch. I released Mommy Dearest and severed one of her daughter's wrists. The kid's hair didn't appreciate that one bit. Seven centipedes snapped from her barrettes and slithered along my fur, searing through my flesh like trickles of boiling water and snaking their way along my back. Her brothers giggled in haunting demonic little spurts, like they were having the time of their undead lives. And because laughing at my royally screwed self wasn't fun enough, the pint-size ghouls continued to stab their claws into my hide while the insects lining their clothing slid from their bodies to join the swarm crawling across me.

I growled and snapped at them, only to fill my jowls with a throng of wriggling bugs. The spirits held tight and their insect army scrambled faster. I swore, knowing I was in serious trouble. If these bugs made their way into my brain, they'd devour me from the inside out and use my soul to raise more dead. *Shit.* Where was a can of Raid when a werewolf needed one?

The centipedes wriggled their way across my thick fur. I

felt every damn movement of their tiny legs as they marched across, burning my flesh. The first squirmed its way into my ear just as the sound of sloshing water reverberated behind me.

Celia, my little hell kitty, gasped behind me. She sprinted forward, holding tight to a giant green pail in her hands. The child spirits hissed at her, this time in alarm. Whatever Celia carried was something they obviously feared.

The contents of her bucket splashed against me, forcing the spooks from my body. The boy who didn't move fast enough hollered with a mind-numbing wail. His clothing scurried away in a frenzy and tunneled into the earth while his body was eaten away by whatever Celia had doused him with. His ribs cracked, one after the other, exposing his rotting and disintegrating organs.

Celia gagged from the reek of his dissolving innards. Luckily, the leftover centipede rammed up my nose conveniently blocked part of the rancid scent.

"Oh God." She swung her pail, sending the spirit's remains soaring into the trunk of an old tree. It exploded in a swarm of flying creepy-crawlies that fell to the forest floor and burrowed deep into the earth.

Back to hell where you belong, asshole.

I lunged at the two remaining kiddos, biting through the spirit boy's neck while Celia severed the little girl's head from her shoulders with a slash of her sharp claws.

"Mama . . . Mama . . . Mama," the decapitated heads cried in garbled and distorted voices before their skulls and bodies caved inward and sank slowly into the earth.

I *changed* back to human and brushed off the drying shells of the remaining centipedes. My puncture wounds started to fill in. They stung like a mo-fo as they sealed. Still, it didn't compare to the pain of rebuilding the half-eaten muscle in my thigh. My flesh seared and my nerves bellowed as the power of my beast restored the bulk of the ravaged area. Slowly the ache receded as the skin knitted closed and reformed a new pink layer.

My wolf's healing ability was one hell of a gift, but not without its agony when it worked that hard and that fast. I pushed the pain deep within me so no more than a grimace wrinkled my features. Outward displays of pain could mark a *were* as weak and get him killed. I hadn't survived this long as a *lone* by being a wimp.

Celia watched the earth reclaim the dead. Her pretty face scrunched when a couple of toadstools sprouted where the ground had swallowed the little buggers. She kicked at them, sending pieces to scatter against the soil. She then bent to retrieve her bucket, careful not to look at me directly. For all the time the *weres* and I had *changed* around her, she'd yet to get used to naked bodies walking around like it was no big deal.

"Holy water?" I asked, pointing to her empty bucket.

She caught my motion in her peripheral vision and nodded. "The wolves have had my sisters keep a couple of buckets on hand since these ghosts have started showing up around Tahoe."

I gritted my teeth as the last pangs of my healing thigh subsided and wiped the sweat off my forehead. "Good idea. Me and the pack have had our share of face-offs with the phantoms and the freaky lately."

Celia smirked. "So have the vamps and I. Just last week, we took out the Jersey Devil. Can you believe that crap?"

I stretched behind her so my regenerated muscle wouldn't tighten up while she continued, and to demonstrate that the healing hadn't wiped me out too bad. If Celia knew how bad I'd hurt moments before, she sure as hell didn't show it. She continued unaffected. "The vamps think a Tribe witch may be using her magic to summon all these spirits—you know, in order to distract us from whatever her demon lord leaders are plotting now."

I kicked out my back leg. "Yeah. The *weres* are under the same assumption. We bashed a couple of skin-walkers into kibble not too far from Mount Rose last Wednesday. Damn, those things are butt ugly."

"You should have seen the Jersey Devil. He was a slobbering mess of half moose, half bear, and reeked like decaying meat." She shuddered. "I can still smell his soiled fur every time I inhale."

My lip curled. "That sucks. The skin-walker had a serious case of leprosy but I've smelled worse. Hell, I even sucked in some of his flaking flesh but thankfully managed to sneeze most of it out."

"Most of it?" Celia grimaced. "Good Lord, Bren. My sister's right. Saving the world sucks serious donkey balls." She motioned around us. "It looks like it was *La Llorona's* turn to play tonight."

"Who?"

"The spirit of the woman you chased down. Latin folklore states she killed her children long ago and now haunts the night in search of them."

"Ah. That's why she was asking where her kids were."

Celia glanced at me before remembering I remained very naked. She quickly looked away. "You understood her? She was speaking in Spanish."

I laughed. "Spirits have a funny way of making themselves heard, Ceel."

"I guess." She kicked at the toadstools that had escaped her wrath. "Although I never expected the little monsters to show up and protect her as viciously as they did. I wish you hadn't chased after her. Aric had Tahoe's head witch reinforce the protective wards around our house. She couldn't have invaded our property if she tried. We could've figured out a way to send her back to the dark realm before her offspring made you their bitch."

"Those little punks didn't make me their bitch!"

She threw her hands in the air. "Bren. I found three very spooky and very dead children with missing eyes and crawling bugs for knickers humping your back and chewing on your ass like bubble gum. Trust me, I've seen better battles."

"I resent that. I was just waiting to make my move."

Celia winked and nodded slowly. "Sure you were, big guy."

I threw an arm around her and hauled her against my side, knowing the last thing she wanted was my hot naked body against hers. She shoved me off, laughing. "Knock it off, Bren."

I tried to grab her again but she leapt out of reach. "For a sexy little thing, you're quite the prude, babe."

She laughed again. "Yeah, the vampires think so, too." She glanced around. "How'd you kill her, anyway?"

"Who?"

"*La Llorona.* I didn't see how you vanquished her."

I stopped smiling, the sense of "oh-shitness" tensing my muscles. "I didn't kill her. I thought you did."

"No . . ." Her head jerked as she scanned the area. "Oh my God. She's still out there. . . . We have to find her—*fast.*"

<h1 style="text-align:center">Chapter Four</h1>

I inhaled long and hard while Celia prowled the perimeter. My nose honed in on a faint trail of rot and torture in the far distance. The sour stench trickled into my nostrils, polluting the otherwise crisp and clean night air. I called to Celia. "She rounded back toward your place."

Once more my beast emerged and tore down the steep mountain. Rocks and debris rolled down from the force of my digging paws. *La Llorona* was a predator in search of prey. She needed a victim. And it looked like she picked Celia's old turf as her place to find one.

Celia's steady steps were barely audible behind me. She was keeping up, even without *changing* into her golden tigress—her secret weapon when she needed the extra muscle. I skidded to a halt when we reached her back lawn. "Where is she—"

A deep hiss cut off Celia's words just my senses alerted me that we'd found her. Aw hell. *La Llorona* scurried like a scorpion up Mrs. Mancuso's house, naked. To her credit, she had quite a fine ass for someone who'd bit it long ago. Although her lolling head where my fangs had mauled and her graying skin did take away from the otherwise sweet view.

I bared my fangs and stalked forward with Celia by my side. A subtle slice through the air signaled my girl's claws were out. Celia was ready. I was ready. And so was *La Llorona's* dress.

I shit you not. The blood red dress pooling at the base of Mrs. Mancuso's deck slithered toward us, ripping into long and lengthening silky ribbons. Rows of little mouths ran from one end of the ribbon to the next . . . screaming.

La Llorona continued to scale the side of the house toward Mrs. M's bedroom unaffected. Me and my wolf couldn't blame her really, not with the devil's prom dress there to protect her. The ribbons snaked my front paws and spiraled up my broad chest and neck from one blink to the next. They squeezed, slowly against my throat while the mouths vocalized their pain. Some shrieked in agony. Others spoke in a haunting echo, soft, sinister, and ghoulish as all hell. I hated what they had to say.

"She murdered me and ate my insides . . . can she eat yours?"

"I like blood," a childlike voice said. "I'll have yours when we kill you . . . if she'll share."

The tiny faces of *La Llorona's* victims pressed against the fabric of the ever lengthening and widening ribbons. My fangs snapped on pure vicious instinct and tore through the fabric, cutting off the voices of the demented and departed. But there was still plenty of dress left.

"Feed me, wolf, I want to taste you. Won't you let me taste you?"

"Tighter," a male with a garbled voice urged, forcing the party dress to cut off my air. "I want to have him . . . and the woman."

His comment to hurt Celia, combined with her terrified screams and growls, set off my wolf like a rabid beast. I roared, tensing my muscles and busting through the noose around my neck. There was no grace, no strategy, or any such bullshit; there was simply my drive to kill those who threatened us and to protect my friend.

My fangs shredded that dress like cornhusks. The cloth wailed in torment as my teeth dug in, the cries weakening and falling silent when the small pieces of fabric flung from my mouth and dropped at my feet.

Celia yanked off the few ribbons enveloping her with her claws and stomped the last little voice asking to suckle blood from her boob. She stood drenched and we were both panting, but the destruction of the dress was not enough to send *La Llorona* back to hell. She'd reached Mrs. Mancuso's window and was clawing on the glass while a couple of roaches spilled from her severed neck. Okay, maybe she wasn't that hot after all.

"I'll get more water," Celia whispered tightly before disappearing into the house.

I rushed forward and catapulted in the air, piercing *La Llorona's* thigh with my fangs. Roaches seeped from the base of her neck like lava and scuttled down her leg and onto my nose. I held tight, using my weight to bring her down. She smacked and pounded on the side of the house and window, trying to keep from falling. I yanked harder, ignoring the storm of bugs raining down. Slowly, I towed her toward the ground, her nails digging into the siding. It sucked, and she tasted like rotting meat. My only relief came from the sound of Celia and her sloshing bucket.

I released her roughly between the first and second floor. Celia flung the holy water against *La Llorona,* burning through the walking dead like acid. *La Llorona* shrieked, melting into gray slime that smelled like man ass . . . just as Mrs. Mancuso flung open her window.

I bolted under Celia's deck. Mrs. M stuck out her curler-ridden head, glancing from the giant smear of evil oozing down her brown siding to Celia and her bucket. "Celia Wird! Did you just throw paint on my house?"

Celia was many things: smart, funny, kind, and beautiful. "Smooth" was sadly not on this gal's list of assets. "Um . . . no?" she said.

I raced around the other side of the house and went in through the front door, laughing my ass off as Mrs. M ripped Celia a new one. As fast as I could I yanked on a pair of sweats Gemini had left in Taran's room and hurried outside, trying my best to put my poker face forward. I grabbed the hose the girls kept out back and tugged it toward Mrs. M's house. Damn, she was a woman possessed, yelling at the top of her lungs with one angry stiff middle finger fully extended. "You and your harlot sisters are nothing but trouble. I'm going to sue. So help me Jesus, I'm going to sue!"

I held out a hand. "It's okay, Mrs. Mancuso. Celia's just

upset I made her memorize Corinthian 629." I really didn't know what the hell I was talking about, but that shit sounded good enough. I nudged Celia back toward her property and started to spray the leftover ghost slime off the house. "Go on, Celia. Go back inside and ask God for forgiveness. And while you're at it, say a couple of Hail Marys and make me a sandwich." I winked at Mrs. Mancuso. "Don't worry, Mrs. M. I'm going to wash the sin off of Celia just like the paint off your house."

"I don't know whether to thank you or smack you," Celia muttered when I strutted back inside.

She stood by her black and tan granite counter, adding a few more slices of cheese to her turkey sandwich. I said "her" because she growled when I tried to snatch it out her hands. "Make your own damn sandwich."

I chuckled and reached for the plate and the fresh loaf of bread she'd left me. "Relax, Ceel, the important thing is we sent evil back to hell and Mrs. M. promised me she wouldn't sue." I sliced more turkey from the leftover Thanksgiving bird and glanced around. "Any pickles?"

She pointed to the row of condiments she'd gathered and finished swallowing. "You know, I thought I was getting better at seeing dark forces at play—considering everything I've been through these past few months. But that crap was just plain freaky." She shuddered. "Did you hear what that little bastard mouth said to me before I crushed it with my boot?"

"About wanting to suckle the blood from your body through your nipple? Yeah. That was some creepy shit right there."

She grimaced and dug into her food. Like me, food was Celia's Zoloft, not to mention we needed to replenish the calories we lost during the brawl. "I hate feeling scared."

I grabbed a couple of beers out of the fridge and set one by Celia's plate. "Then why are you involved, Ceel? You don't have to be a part of this war we're in. Go back to being a nurse. Go back to normal, and hell, find some other guy to give you the damn attention you deserve."

Her lips curved into a sad smile. "You know I can't do that . . . so I use my fear to drive me to kill the things that scare me." She shrugged. "Maybe in helping rid the world of the darkness, someday I won't be so afraid. Besides, it's the right thing to do."

I reached for a handful of chips. "What about the other part?"

She wiped her mouth with a napkin. "Hmmm?"

"Hooking up with someone you can eventually settle down with. Don't look at me like that," I said when her green eyes glimmered with sadness. "Aric can't be with you. You can't be with him. But that doesn't mean you can't be with someone else. It doesn't have to be true love, Ceel. Most humans do just fine with true like."

Celia worked on making us more sandwiches, though it lacked her usual food prep enthusiasm. "You don't understand. I can't picture my life with anyone else. And what if it's true, what if I really am his mate? I know I don't fit into any category of preternatural or human, but doesn't that mean he's my mate, too?"

I stuffed the last bit of my bread in my mouth and reached for the plate she passed me. "Matehood is not all it's cracked up to be, Ceel. My parents were mates. It wasn't enough to save either of them when my father tried to *turn* my mother *were*." I wrapped my knuckles against the cool counter. "Sometimes that love shit is dangerous. Makes you do things you shouldn't."

"You don't want it—to find a mate, I mean?"

No one had ever had the balls to ask me that. Maybe because I chased ass like it was my job and I needed a raise.

"Bren?"

"No. Yes. Well, sometimes." I gripped the bottle of mustard. "I saw what my mom and dad had. Even though I was just a kid, I recognized its significance—its purity, you know?" I shook the mustard bottle hard. Goddamn thing was almost empty. I slammed it on the counter, pissed that none came out even though I wasn't a big fan of mustard. "Emme described matehood as a rare and beautiful thing tonight. Maybe it's too rare, and someone like me doesn't get to have it."

"You don't think you deserve it."

I stopped with the sandwich halfway in my mouth, not lovin' the traces of pity in her voice. "A love like my parents had?" She nodded. "Hell, maybe I don't. But then maybe that's a good thing."

Celia paused. I could see her wrestling with whether to ask her next question. I motioned with my hand, encouraging her to spit it out. "I'm sorry if I'm out of line here, Bren, and you don't have to answer if you don't want to. But why did your dad decide to *turn* your mother? Especially given that you were what? Twelve? The process kills most. They had to know they were risking their lives and your future."

I polished off my sandwich instead of responding right away. Celia must've thought I decided not to answer. She didn't push and resumed her meal.

Only Dan knew the "woe is me" story of my f'd up life. But I knew I could trust this little feline. So I chugged my beer and spilled my guts like a little bitch. "It was my mother's idea." Celia glanced up, surprised by my comment and to hear me answering, I guess. "My dad was a pureblood who was stripped of status and every last dime of his fortune when he abandoned his pack to marry my human mother. She never forgave herself for the losses she caused him." I huffed. "Even though he never blamed her and thought she was the best thing to walk into his life. When I came along, her guilt worsened. She felt like she'd deprived two wolves of their pack." I stared at the empty bag of chips. "The shame was eating her alive . . . so I helped convince my dad that it was the best thing for all of us."

"This wasn't your fault, Bren," Celia said quietly.

I ignored her as the last few moments with my parents flashed in my mind. Her limp and lifeless body crushed beneath his unmoving form, me tugging on their arms, yelling at them to get up, to *breathe,* and begging them not to leave me. I even reminded my dad I had a baseball game. Didn't occur to me my schooling and my life were over.

"You okay?"

I nodded, though it was a damn lie. "You know, Ceel, in my mind I pictured the three of us running through the woods in our beast forms straight into the welcoming embrace of our pack. One big, goddamn family of lupines, panting and wagging our asses off." I laughed bitterly. "Shit. I was such a stupid kid. When they died . . ." I shook my head, a vain effort to wrench the memory of my parents' bodies being loaded into the meat wagon, and cleared my throat for all the good it did me. "After they left me . . . I went to the pack, just like my dad told me to do. He was sure they'd take me in. I was one of them, he'd told me. But the anger my dad's Elders held against him for abandoning them remained. They showed me the door and slammed it behind me. I really thought . . . thought they'd be there for me, you know? And my parents? I thought they'd make it—beat the odds and all that shit." I bowed my head and stared hard at the counter. "Hell, Celia, I've never been more wrong in my life. Those ass-hats wouldn't even give my folks a burial. I never got the chance to say good-bye."

I didn't notice Celia move to my side until she curled her arms around mine and leaned her shoulder against my head. "The decision to *turn* your mother was wrong." She stroked my arm when she felt me tense. "But it came from love, the love your mother had for you and your father. You may have swayed them in that direction—"

"There was no swaying, I damn well pushed!"

"Shhhh." Celia's voice grew quieter. "You only convinced your father because you loved your mother and because her torment hurt you as well. And in your mind, you weren't risking your family, you were looking to expand it, to make it bigger and better."

I shrugged. "I guess. But it still doesn't change shit. Bottom line, I was still left alone. Without parents and without pack."

"And still you survived." She smiled and gave my arm another squeeze. "You're one of the best people I know, Bren."

"Aw hell, Ceel, you need to get out and get to know more people."

She leaned against me but didn't laugh at my comment like I would've liked. "I get now why you were a *lone* wolf for so long. I knew you must have had a good reason, but I never expected your father's former Elders to be so cruel. I can't believe they would abandon one of their own to fend for himself. You were just a little boy."

"What do you expect from pack *weres*? They're all a bunch of stuck-up assholes."

She released me then and regarded me carefully. "Then why join them now after all these years, especially now that *demon* lords are targeting the *weres* for annihilation?"

I reached for my sandwich again. Confessions of a werewolf obviously worked up an appetite. I took a huge chunk out of my sandwich and spoke while I chewed. "This isn't about me, or my grudge toward my dad's Elders. It's about you."

Celia frowned. "Me?"

"Yeah, you. Celia, you're my real pack—you, Dan, your sisters. I had to join the *weres* to help take down the Tribe. I'm not letting them get away with what they did to you and your family."

Celia's lips parted. "You joined Aric's pack because of us?"

"Why else would I have signed up for this Den shit? Because let me tell you, that ex-lover of yours is a ball-busting hard ass. You wouldn't believe the crap he expects me to do."

She watched me closely, I guess waiting for me to say more. I didn't, though, and took another beer out the fridge. "Thank you," she said quietly.

I gave her a stiff nod in response. Hell, Celia would risk her life for me. The least I could do is return the favor. She slipped back to the other side of the counter and resumed eating. "You're not going to end up alone, kid." She swallowed hard at my revelation but then took another bite. "We're going to get married."

That made her smile. "Are we?"

"Totally." I kept munching and popped open a new bag of Doritos. "It'll be an open marriage, of course."

She nodded thoughtfully. "Of course."

"Oh, hell yeah. Dan's eventually going to marry—probably some fugly chick at the rate he's going." I shuddered. "They'll go on to make fugly-ass babies and where will that leave me? Shit, you know I don't cook. And someone has to clean."

"Mmm. Cook *and* clean, too. You really know how to woo a gal."

My grin widened. Ceel was a hell of an audience for all my bullshit. "I'll come home—after a hard night of bartending or banging some hot broad—and you'll be waiting with my breakfast, dressed in an apron and stilettos." I thought about it. "Unless your figure starts to go. Then it might have to be a naughty nurse outfit—just to cover some of that sagging shit up. It's the perfect arrangement. What do you say?"

"Oh, hot damn and golly, Bren, who could resist such a generous offer?"

I would have believed her if she hadn't nailed me in the head with an apple from the fruit bowl. I caught it on the rebound and took a bite. "Thanks, Ceel."

We finished our sandwiches while continuing to rip into each other, had a couple more, and washed them down with a blackberry pie. "Do you want me to pick you up, or do you just want me to meet you at the club?"

Celia licked the last trace of blackberry goodness off her top lip. "You still want to go out? After what we just went through outside?"

I grinned. "A bet's a bet. Besides, you can't let a bunch of spooks ruin your good time."

"I guess." Celia stiffened before her head whipped toward the sliding glass doors leading out to her deck. She rushed to the doors. I followed, my wolf sensing something stirring outside. "Oh . . . my God."

I slung an arm around her shoulders when I saw what had her lids peeling back. Wisps and shimmering veils of silver and white lifted from where we'd pimp-slapped *La Llorona* back to hell, and from where the shreds of screeching fabric had met their end. One by one, thirty, forty, maybe fifty ghosts swirled their way into the sky. "Huh. Well, will you look at that?"

She slowly turned her head to face me. "There's an army of ghosts taking off to the moon in my backyard, and this is seriously all you have to say?"

"Relax, Ceel, this is a good thing. It means we shattered whatever nasty magic trapped *La Llorona's* victims in her dress and compelled them to want to devour our blood and guts. Given how long she's been prowling the earth, it probably took some time for her power to fully dissolve." I pointed upward. "Her victims are free now and have a one-way ticket up to the pearly gates, babe. So, we going out?"

She smiled, watching the spirits drift away. "Yeah, sure. I guess we have reason to celebrate." She jumped when the transparent image of a little boy skipped barefoot up to the glass door. Big eyes blinked back and an even bigger grin greeted Celia. He waved at her with his little hands. Celia waved back and chuckled when the little boy blew her a kiss.

We watched as his little body elongated into one long swirl that joined the others spiraling into the sky.

I tugged Celia against me and whispered into her ear. "Hey, Ceel. Do you think that was the little puke who wanted a sip from your boob?"

<h1 style="text-align:center">Chapter Five</h1>

After a quick shower back at my place, I met Celia at the Watering Hole. The music blared and the colored lights flashed to the beat of some Lady Gaga song. I found Celia dancing on the floor, surrounded by a cluster of Misha's vamps who dressed like naughty Catholic schoolgirls. I rolled my eyes. That master vamp asshole she was shacking up with wanted her watched closely.

Celia had changed from her sweaty, evil-ghost-smeared clothes into a sheer white top with a tight little black camisole underneath. Her jeans were dark and her boots black. Anyone would think she dressed for style. Nah, it was all about comfort.

I watched her for a while. That gal was well aware of her body and how to move it. Aric and her must've had a hell of a time together. It sucked that no one paid attention to her now. As always, humans gave her ample space. A tiger's presence had that effect.

Celia inched her way from the group when two of the naughty Catholics began to dance provocatively against each other. Shit like that made her uncomfortable. The vamps didn't care. It was always all about *them*. More attention meant more power—power over humans who begged to have sex with them. The vamps obliged them willingly, getting laid left and right, while they pierced their prey with their fangs and took small amounts of blood.

The one with the pigtails and little librarian glasses laughed when the chick with long black hair flicked her tongue on her plunging neckline. My hate for vamps aside, it was kind of hot. They continued to grind, garnering the lustful stares of patrons and basking in the attention. I guessed the tiny little uniforms weren't enough to get the interest they desired . . . nor the pheromones they emitted each time they breathed.

Like a row of falling dominos, males popped wood around the scantily clad vamps. Celia did a double-take, scenting their arousal. She backed away, right into some asshole trying to snap a picture of the gyrating vamps with his cell phone. The loser dropped his phone and stumbled backward when he caught Celia's defensive posture and uneasy expression. She lowered her gaze to appear less threatening. It didn't work. The guy continued to back away, leaving his cell phone on the floor where some bigger dude mashed it with his foot.

Celia crossed her arms and left the floor. I knew what she was thinking, that her looks had scared him. *No, babe. That would be that little feline you keep closely in check.*

Celia didn't get how beautiful she was—long sexy hair, large green eyes that saw right through you, and a killer body anyone with a libido would drag off to bed. Aric never could keep his eyes off of her . . . what blows is neither could that bloodsucker, Misha. Both had managed to get close to her, but only because *weres* and vamps didn't scare easily. Problem was Misha was getting a little too close now.

The sea of bodies parted as I advanced toward Celia. I had the power to draw back my beast just enough to blend in among humans, a trick I'd learned being *lone*. I never needed that extra aggression. My height and bulk was enough for humans to back the hell up. I hurried along, and just to give her a little love, grabbed Celia's ass like it was on sale.

She slipped out of my sight before I could blink and appeared behind me, rewarding my oh-so-loving touch with a ferocious wedgie.

"Ow! What the hell was that for?"

Celia released enough of my boxers so one of my boys slipped back in place. "You grabbed my butt."

"I was just being affectionate! Let go so I can still knock

up some lucky gal one day."

She tugged one last time for emphasis then released. I whirled around and tried to coax the gang out of my stomach and back home to the front of my pants. "Damn, Ceel, you could've cost me a few pups."

"You seriously want to have kids?"

I yanked my black T-shirt out of my jeans just to give my crew a little more breathing room and smirked. "You seem surprised."

She played with the edges of her long mane. "It's not that I don't think you'd make a good dad, but you're such a hound, I never thought you'd consider settling down."

I clasped her hand and pulled her to me. "Who said anything about settling down?" I dipped her and planted a raspberry on her neck. She laughed and pushed me away. It was all in good fun. Damn shame Misha's vampires didn't appreciate my awesome sense of humor.

The four she-vamps abandoned their meals and stormed to us. Within seconds they had us surrounded, their hisses sharp enough to slice the club air thick with sweat and lust. An icy blonde extended her nails and snarled. "Is this mongrel bothering you, Celia?"

Celia stepped between us. "No, Liz. You know Bren's my buddy."

Liz lowered her lids, her tone dangerous. "The master wouldn't appreciate him fondling what's his."

My grin widened. "That wasn't a fondle. That was a kiss." I shrugged. "I fondled her ass before the smooch, but you sluts missed it since you were staking out your next meal."

"Let me make myself clear." Celia's glare fixed on the blonde. "I don't belong to Misha, and my friends are not to be touched."

The vamps took Celia's growls out on me. They circled slowly like a clan of hyenas, donning stilettos sharp enough to puncture a sternum. I laughed without humor. Maybe that was the point in their choice of footwear. I flexed for them. What could I say? I was one classy mo-fo. "That's right, sweethearts. You only wish you could touch this." I waved them off. "Now run along and gather up some virgins."

"Bren is who I came to meet," Celia said when one of the vamps advanced. "I want to spend time alone with him. I'll catch up with you after you . . . ah, eat." The vamps hesitated when Celia made it clear it was time to scat. She sighed. "That's an order," she mumbled, as if embarrassed to give a direct command.

The icy blonde nodded and slowly sashayed her way back to where the throng of idiots pitching tents anxiously awaited the vamps' return. The others followed, one after the other, except for the naughty Catholic with the jet black hair—the one with the long flickering tongue. Not that I'd noticed. She slinked her way to me. She was tall to begin with, but the thigh-high boots she wore left her face just a few inches below mine.

"*Edith Anne*," Celia warned.

"Just saying good-bye to your pet, Celia," she answered with a phony pout, not bothering to glance her way. She licked her overly glossed lips and ran the nail of her middle finger down the length of my nose, speaking in a tone that suggested sex and slaughter all in one breath. "A word of warning, little doggie. Some things are dangerous if you touch."

I snapped her nail off with my teeth and spit it on the floor. "You got that much right, sweetheart."

Fury flared behind her coal-black eyes and her incisors elongated to fall past her collagen-injected lips. For a second, I thought my wolf would get a chance to play again. My lip curled. *I've got chompers too, bat-girl.* She disappointed me by backing away, her glare telling me she'd prefer to take my wolf up on his challenge.

"Remind me to tell Misha how well you follow orders, Edith."

Celia's threat broke Edith's eye contact with me. She quickened her steps and joined the others, her hips swinging hard enough to smack a baseball into left field. Not that I was watching or anything. "Is she wearing panties, Ceel?"

Celia groaned. "I don't know. I don't care. But knowing Edith, probably not."

The she-vamps returned to jiggling their cleavage like world hunger depended on it. "Friends of yours?"

Celia chuckled. "Hardly. They barely tolerate me, but I'm not working for Misha to win a popularity contest."

I clasped her hand and led to the bar. "So, why'd you bring them?" I bounced and bartended at the Hole Thursday night through Saturday for extra bucks. My pal, Ed, was mixing drinks that night. He saw me coming and immediately dropped a bucket of Coronas on the bar for us, shoving limes down the long necks just like I liked them. "Thanks, Ed."

Celia sat on the stool next to me and crossed her legs. "I didn't bring them. Misha popped a blood vessel when I told him about our tussle with *La Llorona* and her babies." She lifted a beer from the bucket and motioned with it to the dance floor. "I give you my bodyguards for the night."

The vamp with the pigtails wrapped her legs around some frat boy and rode him like a Budweiser Clydesdale. His buddies whooped and pumped their fists, oblivious to the fact their pal was just another morsel with legs. I laughed. "That's one hell of a team you got there, Ceel. Can I request their services next time my body needs a guardin'?"

"Believe me, I tried to ditch them, but they shadowed me here."

I took a long pull of my beer. "Freak-ass spirit or not, your buds there would've come along. Misha doesn't strike me as the trusting sort. Betcha my next paycheck he wants to keep an eye on you."

"You're right. But he means well enough." She took another glance at the good Catholics. "Despite who he insists watches out for me."

A word to the wise: never trust a vampire. "Ceel, I don't like how chummy you and that prick are getting. Vamps are only out for themselves. Whatever the hell is going on between you two, don't fool yourself into thinking Misha's more than he is or that he wouldn't throw you to a pride of werelions to save his ass."

"I'm not stupid, Bren. I know Misha's out for Misha." Celia wouldn't look at me when she spoke; instead she stared off into the crowd of sweat-soaked and dancing bodies. "But he's not so bad. He does have a heart."

I swore in my head, not crazy about her growing

endearment toward the idiot. I hated her living with Misha. Hell, I hated her talking to him, but I knew better than to push. Unlike most others I could've intimidated, Celia pushed back—*hard*. For all five feet three, she was a strong little thing.

"So why are the she-vamps dressed in those uniforms?" I asked in order to change the subject.

"They always dress like that." She shrugged and tried to hide her smirk. "Misha says it's because they're good Catholics."

I finished my bottle and reached for another when Celia jumped hard enough to slosh her beer across her dark jeans. Her eyes widened as they cut through the crowd and fixed on the steps leading down to the dance floor and, good *God* . . . I almost shit myself.

Dan. My roommate. My buddy. My BFF for life looked as if he'd been attacked by a mob of John Travoltas.

He took in the sea of bodies below him and bounced his head—off beat mind you—to some Maroon Five remix as if gathering his courage. And hell, he needed it to survive the catastrophic getup hugging his skinny ass and scrawny form.

Celia blinked, watching Dan's head bop and zigzag on his shoulders like a rooster in midstride. "Is that . . . is that a leisure suit he's wearing?" she managed to spit out. I nodded like a dumbass, still mesmerized by the amount of polyester covering his body. "Are . . ." she swallowed hard. "Are the seventies, like, back?"

She wasn't asking me. She was begging me to tell her yes. "If they are, I'm going to track the asshole who brought 'em back and beat his ass."

Dan adjusted the extra wide lapels of his baby blue suit and smoothed the collar of his matching silk shirt. Jesus, he even had a paisley hanky shoved into his breast pocket.

And because the look didn't scream "I've never had my cherry popped and never will" hard enough, Dan had attempted to slick back the Brillo pad of curls he called hair.

The hair flattened out on the sides but only partially on top. Fantastic. All he'd managed to do was mullet his ass. His face lit up and he waved when he saw us.

Celia clasped her hand over her mouth in horror. "You can't do this to him, Bren. You can't have him try to get laid in this . . . *ensemble*."

Humor drove through the stupefied repulsion Dan's suit had caused and fired its way onto my face. "Heh, heh." My shoulders shook. "Heh, heh, heh." Celia elbowed me hard as Dan drew closer. The dancers paused mid-shimmy just to gape and point—and laughed out loud when he almost tripped over the hem of his bell-bottoms.

"Heh, heh, heh, heh."

"Don't laugh, Bren," Celia insisted. "Whatever you do, do *not* laugh at— Oh hey, Danny!"

I busted out laughing; no man should ever wear that many dyed chemicals on his skin. Hell, I could almost see him getting cancer.

Dan stopped short and pushed his sliding glasses back up his nose. "What's so funny?"

"You, man. It looks like Sonny Bono threw up on you." I took another swig of my beer and almost choked on his puzzled reaction. "Shit, Dan, how the hell are you going to get some ass in this monstrosity?"

"It's not about the clothes, it's about the attention they'll bring me." He shoved the hanky further into his pocket. "Research shows getting noticed is the first step to meeting someone, and that more flashy attire keeps attention focused on you. Besides, it's a nice suit. I paid a lot of money for it."

Celia forced a smile. "The blue does bring out your olive skin and brown eyes."

I nodded in agreement. "It also screams 'I'm a virgin and will blow you for fashion advice.' " I handed him a Corona. "I'll tell you what, Dan. You get laid tonight, in that suit, and I'll throw in next month's rent." I pointed at him. "And to sweeten the deal, I'm not even holding 'hot chick' as a requirement. Semi-attractive and not blind is good enough."

Just then, a semi-attractive, not blind redhead in a striped tube top snaked her way to the bar and ordered some girly drink in a pineapple. *Here's your chance,* I mouthed to Dan.

Dan and his suit leaned against the bar. "Here, let me buy you a drink."

The gal's lids flickered, probably temporarily blinded by the color of Dan's attire. But then she shocked the hell out of me when her lips parted into a smile. "How about two?"

Dan smiled back at her and motioned to the bartender . . . and while he paid for the drinks the chick walked away with her drink and his. She hurried her way back to where some idiot waited, and handed him Dan's drink. He smiled and waved after Tube Top said something to him and motioned our way.

Dan cleared his throat. "Um, looks like she's with someone."

I slung around him. "Don't worry, Dan. You did a good thing. That poor bastard was probably thirsty."

As the night went on, Dan struck out left and right. Celia asked him to dance twice. Both times he turned her down. She walked away shaking her head and made her way back to me. My hands slipped around her waist and I pulled her onto my lap just as one of Misha's vampires passed by. The vamp narrowed her gaze through her tiny librarian glasses and hissed. I swatted at the air as if batting a fly. "Don't you have someone to eat? Go away."

"Agnes Concepcion, please. I told you he's just a friend. Go back to the others." Celia watched her until she disappeared into the growing numbers taking up the dance floor. We were already at capacity, the bouncers on duty letting too many clubbers in. "It's getting too crowded and my tigress is on edge. Do you want to call it a night?"

"Nah. I need to keep an eye on Dan. What was his excuse for not dancing with you? It might have worked to his advantage to be seen with a cutie like you."

She gave me a small smile. "He said he's afraid that if he dances with me, it'll ruin his chance to hook up."

"Did you tell him his suit has already done that for him?"

She laughed. "No, I didn't want to hurt—"

Celia tensed as my hackles rose. A sudden chill overtook the air around us. She slipped off my lap. I stood, releasing the throaty growl rumbling my chest. Gray mist crept its way from the exits and crawled along the floor, thick enough to blanket the feet of the dancing patrons. The humans continued to bump and glide against each other, their steps growing louder as the music faded and the hairs on my arms curled tight against my skin.

The air grew denser, tightening my chest. Something had entered the club from all directions. I didn't know what the hell it was, but knew we needed to get rid of it—fast.

"Do you feel that?" Celia whispered.

I nodded and motioned to the vamps. They'd stopped dancing and straightened, their keen sights taking everything in. "Your girlfriends felt it, too."

"Can you tell what we're dealing with?"

"No. But it's nothing good. Looks like the spirits aren't done for the night."

Chapter Six

Celia pulled a cell phone out of her back pocket. "My phone's dead. How about yours?"

I yanked out mine. "Yeah. The paranormal activity must be interfering with the electrical equipment." The flashing strobe lights flickered in and out and music reached an abrupt end. I reached for her hand again. "Come on, let's take a look around."

We made our way through the crowd of sweating bodies. Celia stopped and tugged on my arm. "Bren, look."

I hadn't noticed the clubbers' eyes. They stared expressionless at their partners, despite how hard their bodies moved against each other and to a beat of the music that no longer played. "Shit. Their souls have been numbed."

"What?"

"A poisonous spirit can paralyze a weak soul—especially if their prey is intoxicated. Think of a snake that's bitten a rat. Makes the rat easier to eat."

"Jesus," Celia whispered taking in the swarm of drunk humans. "There are a lot of rats around here."

Speaking of which. The she-vamps slinked their way around the bodies, charging to Celia's side. "We have to get you out of here."

The icy blonde reached for Celia but withdrew when Celia hissed. "I'm not going anywhere until we dispose of whatever entity has trapped the humans."

Blond bombshell shook her head. "We'll deal with it once we get you back to the master."

"No. It'll take too long. I'm not risking some poor sap having his soul devoured." Celia's husky tone was absolute and she squared her jaw. "I'm staying to help Bren. And so are you."

The blonde swore before whirling to face the chick with the dark pigtails and little glasses. "What are we dealing with here, Agnes?"

Agnes frowned. "I won't know until we find it. It, they—whatever the hell is scattered around. We have to wait until one takes physical form to feed. It'll entice the others to present in their physical forms and feast."

"We have to wait until it chooses its prey?" Celia's head whipped around. "Aw hell, there's got to be a hundred people crammed in here." She prowled toward the center. "Spread out in pairs. Bren, you're with me."

I pounded after her and almost ran her down when she stopped short. A stunning Latina with skin the color of warm chocolate and long black hair that dragged to her feet stood swaying in the middle of the floor watching Dan. His eyes remained partly in focus; unlike the other fools surrounding him, he wasn't drunk, and therefore not trapped in the spirits' magic. He was, however, making an ass out of himself. In a mad effort to "wow," Dan had thrown common sense, pride, and his balls out the window. There he stood in perfect nerd glory: one hand clasped behind his neck, the other square in front of him jerking erratically. He was, no lie, trying to impress the hot babe by doing the "the sprinkler." If I wasn't busy trying to find the evil that continued to burn my senses, I'd have slapped the shit right out of him.

The Latina's head whipped in our direction, fast enough to toss the blanket of hair shrouding her naked form behind her. Black, unearthly, immortal eyes blinked back at us. She bared her jagged teeth and snarled, "*Mine.*"

Oh, *hell* no.

Dan's hands dropped to his sides and his face blanched. Me and Ceel shoved aside a few bodies and bolted to him. "*Get back, Dan!*" I growled.

Celia disappeared in a blur of speed. My steps grew

heavy, weaker, despite how hard and fast I tried to propel my body forward. The thick air solidified in my chest, smothering my wolf and forcing him to lose consciousness. I fought to stay alert and lift my feet while coaxing my beast to wake and rise.

The mist slithered up my thighs, morphing my muscles into lead and pulling them from my bones. I groaned from the strain. And still I pushed. I had to destroy the spirit. She'd chosen Dan. I had to save him . . .

A trumpet blasted and a second Latina stepped in front of me. *Good God.* This one was younger, no more than twenty, and the most beautiful being I'd ever laid eyes on. The muffled crunch of a fist meeting hard bone made me want to tear my gaze away from her. Someone . . . some*thing* screeched in agony as skin was punctured and sliced like beef. I thought I picked up Celia's pained grunt. And still I kept my focus on the vision of sex and desire before me. The fight—or whatever was happening ahead of us—didn't matter. Nothing did. The lovely lady standing before me became my world.

Long dark ringlets curved around her heart-shaped face and the swell of her breasts. Brown perfect nipples punctured like bullets through the sheer fabric of her white dress. She ran a hand between her legs and rubbed, adding enough friction to make her lids flutter.

She was offering herself to me. And who was I to deny her? We needed our bodies to join. It was the only way. The only way to end her suffering . . . and mine.

"*Bren!*" Celia flung herself at my love.

My love answered by punching her in the jaw and sending her reeling into me. I snatched Celia's wrists with one of my hands when she lurched back to attack. She fought my hold, screaming, "Damn it, Bren, snap out of it!"

The woman approached me slowly, her smile widening and her nipples taunting me to play. I jerked Celia to the side, extending my arm to keep her away from us and giving my lovely beauty space to work. She yanked my T-shirt over my head and flicked her tongue down my chest and toward the strain pounding against my jeans. Celia lurched forward and kicked her in the stomach, despite my best efforts to keep her still. My love responded with a growl then ignored Celia to return to me.

The room darkened as she unbuckled my belt. All I saw was her, my entire being mesmerized by the sultriness behind those large brown eyes. The desire to have her mouth around me consumed me. I yanked the waistband of my jeans, helping her to pull them down.

Celia twisted and wrenched her body. I forgot she was there fighting me and became only partially aware that she'd begun to jerk away from us. Instead I focused on my lovely admirer and how she latched onto my boxers and pulled them down with her pretty pointed teeth.

Pointed teeth?

She licked me again . . . with her long gray tongue.

Gray tongue?

My wolf jolted awake, howling inside me and insisting something was wrong. I think he also called me a horny moron, but I might've misheard.

My beast's rage shot to the surface. I could sense his growls, demanding to be released. Odd considering I was about to get some head . . . from a gal with pointy teeth and a gray tongue. *What the—*

Something cold hit my crotch; smacking me out of my stupor.

Celia had dumped an entire pitcher of beer on Little Bren. My hands slapped to my sides, releasing Celia and, son of a bitch, did she ever lose her shit. She nailed the Latina with a spinning back kick to the head. The woman whirled in the air and crashed with a hard thud on the concrete floor. Her skirt flew upward, exposing one gray leg and another shaped like some strange-ass kitchen utensil made of wood.

The spirit kicked out her leg, nailing Celia hard in the stomach. I lunged at them but failed to move anything but my arms. My body jerked viciously and my muscles strained from the effort. I remained stuck, watching and helpless to stop the devil's version of Martha Stewart from taking on my friend.

What the hell?

Celia and the freak rolled around me, toppling the patrons now frozen in place. And they weren't the only ones brawling to the death. Misha's vampires battled bare-ass-naked women whose skin alternated from shades of brown to dark blue.

Despite their malevolence and thirst for blood, the spirits' exotic beauty proved hard to ignore. Their lovely faces drew me to them, and so did their aroma of sin and sex. Whatever they were had the same power to lure me, just like the one Celia had stopped from going down on me.

Instead of kitchen utensils for legs, the vamps' opponents kicked with backward facing feet. Their long hair whipped around as they wrestled and clawed at the Catholic schoolgirls. The vamps grunted and screamed. Their opponents chirped like exotic birds. It was all kinds of hot and would've made one hell of a porno. Too bad these porn stars wanted to munch on my soul like pretzels.

Edith Anne, the Catholic with the crazy long tongue, let out a scream and slammed one of the spirits into the floor. She straddled her and hammered her fist repeatedly into the spirit's skull until black blood smeared her white shirt and the spirit's body buckled inward.

The vamp with the librarian glasses cleaved into another spirit's stomach and yanked out rows of decaying bowels. I continued to catch portions of the action as the vamps bashed into the entities. They held their own and then some. Thankfully, so did my girl Celia.

The freak Celia fought tried to kick her with her wooden limb. Celia was ready for her. She locked onto the leg with her arm and belted it with the heel of her foot. The spirit shrieked. A loud snap followed by splintering wood signaled the abrupt loss of her bizarre and creepy-ass appendage. It also provided Celia with one hell of a weapon. She lifted the cracked piece and stabbed it through the spirit's chest. The spirit bolted up, releasing a flow of gray foam from her mouth and slicing her wicked nails at Celia. Celia scrambled behind her, yanking back the entity's hair and using her claws to sever the spirit's head.

Blood the color of concrete splashed me across the face and bare chest. Celia held the head of her opponent, scowling at me.

"What?" I asked defensively. "I'm numb from the waist down."

Celia gave Little Bren a quick glance, her voice less than patient when she spoke. "That's not what it looked like to me."

She tossed the demon's head aside just as Misha's vampires hurried to her. "Did we get them all?"

The naughty librarian/even naughtier Catholic schoolgirl wiped her bowel-smeared hands on the back of some guy's shirt. "Yes. The trance should lift soon."

Celia watched the mist recede into the spirits as their bodies bubbled and frothed. "What were those things, Agnes?"

Agnes adjusted her cleavage before she began rebraiding her long pigtails. For a vamp, she had her priorities straight. She motioned behind her to where the body she had fun disemboweling had begun to disintegrate. "*Ciguapas*. They're Dominican. They're said to lure men into the forests to have sex with them."

I shrugged. "That doesn't sound so bad."

That earned me a smile from Agnes. "No, but then they kill them afterwards." Her smile widened. "Slowly. Sometimes even over weeks."

Celia pointed to the one with the leg found in the culinary section. "What about that one?" She jerked back when the abandoned head popped, fizzled, and crumpled inward.

Agnes eyed the cracked limb as it began to char and crumble. "That's *La Tunda*. She's Colombian and downright nasty."

Celia shuddered. "Yeah. That wooden leg is hideous."

"It is," Agnes agreed, stepping back and adjusting her tiny glasses. "But that's not what I meant by nasty. She emits a gas by breaking wind in order to keep her victims docile and dazed."

"Ew," the rest of us said. Hell, I guess that explained the blasting trumpet. "I told you I couldn't move," I mumbled to Celia.

Celia threw her hands out. "Then how come the vampires and I could?"

Agnes watched me fix my pants. "*La Tunda's* powers don't work on supernatural beings. Unless, of course, they're easily influenced." She giggled. "Or aroused."

Celia pushed her hair away from her face. "Well, the important thing is that they're back to blazes where they belong." She lifted a few of the swaying bodies off the floor when they started to stir and the music exploded over the speakers. "Help me get them up, and be sure to alter their memories. They're starting to wake up and God only knows what they saw."

I hoisted a few off their feet, pausing when one of the vamps stopped for a bite. "Edith, cut it out!"

She scowled at Celia and took one last defiant lick. "What? I haven't eaten all night and I'm thirsty, damn it."

Celia opened her mouth to say something to her, but then stopped suddenly. Her head whipped around. "Bren, where's Danny?"

I straightened and veered behind me. His scent failed to reach my senses. "The last time I saw him, he was with the naked chick you took out."

Celia urged the vamps forward. "Find him. Make sure he's okay."

We raced around the dance floor in a mad rush, searching for any trace of his scent. My feet pounded down the hall toward the bathrooms. I threw opened the doors. "Dan. Dan! Are you in here, man?" Silence was my only response. Shit, was it too much to hope he was hiding in a stall?

Celia sprinted up behind me. "He's not in any of the offices, and the vamps can't find him anywhere."

I backed out of the bathroom and froze. My nose fixed onto a faint trickle of Dan's obnoxious cologne. It trailed in the direction of the emergency exit down the dark hall. I bolted toward it and latched on to the smell. The alarm blasted as I barreled through the door with Celia hot on my heels.

The air in the alley mixed with the rotting garbage from the dumpster and still I scented Dan's musky cologne . . . and drops of his blood.

"He's been taken," I growled.

Chapter Seven

According to Agnes, legend states that a *Ciguapa* can only be tracked by a black and white dog, with extra digits, during a full moon.

Well, screw that. The full moon wasn't until the next night and no one I knew had any extra fingers. That wouldn't stop me. I may have been a loafer, but I was the best damn tracker in California.

I punched Aric's number on speed dial when Celia ran off to get her Lexus. The reception was shitty at best. We obviously hadn't destroyed all the damn spirits. Their dark energy continued to interfere with the reception. Aric answered on the first ring, and surprise, surprise, he was pissed as all hell and growling. *"Did you send a wereskunk to gas bomb my Warriors' cars?"*

"Dan's been taken," I said in way of a response. "We're at the Hole. A bunch of Latin ghosts showed up and wreaked havoc. We destroyed the few we saw, but there must've been more."

Screams from the club cut me off. "What's happening?" Aric pressed.

I poked my head inside. "The humans here are waking up and I think someone stepped on a melting head. Don't worry. The vamps are on it."

Suspicion lowered Aric's voice. "What are you doing

with vamps at the Hole?"

I debated whether to tell him. In the end, I knew there was no way around it. "They shadowed Celia. She's with me."

"I see." Aric paused briefly before switching into Leader mode. "I'm sending a team to scout the area in case there's more spirits seeking to feast. *Stay. There.* The Warriors will help you track Dan."

Celia screeched her car to a halt along the curve and flung open the passenger door. I hauled ass toward it. "Sorry. No can do. The trail's getting cold." I jumped in, immediately lowering the window and sticking my head out. In the distance I caught the exhaust from Dan's car. He needed a new muffler. *Perfect.* My nose locked on the stench. The hunt was on.

"Bren, don't fight me on this. You don't know what we're dealing with. You're no good to Dan if you get your own soul devoured. Wait for backup!"

Celia stiffened when she caught Aric's voice, but stomped on the accelerator when I pointed down the street. "I have backup. Celia's with me."

Aric swore. "Tell her I don't want her involved."

Celia narrowed her eyes at my phone and continued to drive. "I'm not letting Bren track Danny alone, Aric."

His tone softened. He'd heard her. "Celia, it's too dangerous. I don't want anything to happen to you."

"And I don't want anything to happen to Danny," she insisted.

"I know, love. But I have a pack of wolves ready to help you. Just give them time to get there."

Celia released a shaky breath. Must have been the "love" comment. *Smooth, Alpha asshole, real goddamn smooth.* She collected herself and tried to reason with him. "There's no time to waste, Aric. We need to find Danny, and we need to find him fast. These ghosts—they're hungry. And right now, Danny's their only meal."

"Celia, please don't do this without me."

Her eyes focused hard on the road as she ignored him. "Which way now?" she asked when we reached the intersection.

"Left," I answered after drawing in more air.

"Celia—"

I cut Aric off. "Looks like she's listening to you about as much as she did when you were together. Later, boss. I'll *call* when I'm onto something."

Aric snarled another curse before I could disconnect. I took another whiff. "Go up 431. It looks like they're headed toward Mount Rose." My phone rang. I tossed it in the glove compartment and lifted my body out of the car to sit on rim of the door.

Celia's phone rang next. "Crap. It's Aric." The ringer abruptly cut off. I thought she answered until she hit a few buttons and nothing happened. "We must be getting closer. My phone's dead again."

"Or the collected spirits are more than we thought," I muttered.

I continued to hang out the car window to track the sour stench of Dan's muffler. The rows of cedar-planked homes disappeared one by one until the thickening woods swallowed us like an approaching army. I slipped back into the cabin when the only aroma interfering with the cold autumn night was the lingering exhaust of Dan's muffler.

"This is all my goddamn fault."

Celia's eyes cut from the long winding road. "It's not. You're not the one calling forth these ghosts to rise. We need to find out who it is and shut her trap."

"But Dan wouldn't be here if I hadn't bet he couldn't land a decent lay."

"Danny knows what you're like—we all do." Her voice quieted. "That doesn't mean he doesn't know you care." Celia pulled on her smeared lacey shirt. The gray blood was plastered all over it. She ripped it from her body in one hard tug and tossed it in the backseat, leaving only the skimpy black top beneath. I barely noticed how it hugged her full breasts. My focus remained on finding Dan.

"I bust his balls too much."

Celia smirked. "Ball busting is your calling card. Hell, it's practically your middle, last, and confirmation name." She patted my knee. "We'll find him, Bren."

"I just don't want to find him in pieces." I took another whiff. "I smelled his blood in the alley. Shit, I can smell some in the air now."

Celia clenched her jaw. "I know. I scented it, too. I don't smell anything now." She sighed. "These things need him. If they wanted him dead . . . we would've found him already."

She meant to say, we would've found his body ditched in the alley. I knew it because damn it all, I was thinking it, too.

When I met Dan, I was working at a gym in Palo Alto as a personal trainer. Cake job; I didn't even need to work out. My beast gave the false appearance that I survived on protein shakes and spent every waking moment lifting. All I had to do was pretend like I could make some skinny ass wimp look like me by convincing him to buy the shit the gym sold to build bulk . . . along with locking him into a six month membership. The first wimp sent my way was Dan.

We tried squats first, just to loosen his spaghetti limbs. He face planted within the first four and cracked his glasses. A few of the meatheads watching laughed. I didn't, and half expected him to bolt from the humiliation. I would have. Instead the little turd wiped the blood from his nose and fixed his glasses. "Um. What's next?" he asked me.

"A trip to the emergency room," I answered him honestly.

He ignored me and moved toward the weights. I followed and maneuvered him back to the rowing machine where I'd thought he wouldn't get hurt. Hell, the motions were too much for him. He flailed around as if drowning. Hands-down the most uncoordinated piece of work I'd ever seen. Somehow he managed to belt himself in the schnoz with his knee. I yanked him up by his now bloody shirt and tossed him a towel . . . which he of course, didn't catch.

The others laughed. They stopped laughing at the sight of my glare. I crossed my arms and loomed over Dan. He blinked up at me with his shattered lenses. Damn. He probably saw twelve of me. "Why are you here?"

He glanced around. "To get in shape."

I didn't need to take a whiff to know he was lying. "Sure you are. Why are you here?" I asked again.

He lowered the towel from his battered nose. "I want to look better so I can meet women."

I nodded. "You want to get laid."

His face heated and he backed away, pointing to the display cabinet. "Will this, ah, help? You know, build more muscle?"

"Nope. It'll just make you crap out your left lung." I motioned around. "None of this shit is going to help you. You can't squat worth a crap, and anything above fifty pounds might kill you. Don't waste your time. Don't waste your cash. Get the hell out of here and find some nice librarian to bang."

The gym fell silent. Funny thing about your first week of work, the boss was always watching. She stormed out in the middle of some Pilates class and fired me on the spot. Fine by me. She was a lousy lay and her place smelled like moldy jock straps. Dan chased me to my car after I yanked off my official gym T-shirt and tossed it on the floor on my way out. "Sir, wait!"

I opened the door to my POS Camaro and slipped inside, slamming the door so the rusted lock would catch. The engine coughed, sputtered, and finally caught. I sighed when I realized Dan was lurking by my door, his glasses just barely hanging onto his face. I rolled down the window. "The name's Bren. You call me 'sir' again and I'll beat your ass."

Dan's shoulders slumped. "Sorry. I didn't mean . . . you were honest in there." He hooked a thumb behind him toward the gym, as if I didn't know where he'd meant. He lowered his head. "You also didn't laugh when the others did. That was, you know, cool."

Blood smudged his nose. The afro on the top of his head was more Bozo than Tito. And his thin frame was one false move away from shattering. He looked like a clown that had been run out of circus school for embarrassing the profession.

And he was thanking me for being nice.

It wasn't hard to tell he'd been dumped on. And hell, couldn't I relate? I huffed. "Get in."

"Huh?"

I jerked my head and grinned, something telling me I was in for one hell of a time. "I said get in, Stan."

"It's Dan . . . Dan Matagrano." He walked slowly around

the car and climbed in. "Where are we going?"

"To get you laid," I said before put-put-puttering out of the parking lot.

"He just wanted to get laid," I said out loud to Celia.

"What?" She'd been playing with her blue tooth, trying to call her sisters for help. White noise blared out of the speakers the more she fumbled with the touch screen.

"Dan. When we met. Even then he just wanted to get laid."

Celia shook her head. "No. I just think he wanted to stop feeling so lonely. It was a hard time for him then. He was finishing up at Stanford and the competition was cutthroat."

I laughed without humor. "So he said. Pricks. His fellow graduates were always trying to sabotage his work. At least I helped him by getting him some tail."

"You're wrong, Bren." Celia smiled sadly. "You helped him by becoming his best friend. Yes, you pick on him. Yes, you give him a hard time. But you'd crush anyone to bloody rubble who tried to hurt him." She pursed her lips. "And don't ever think he doesn't know that."

I nodded hoping she was right only to abruptly straighten when we rounded the curve and the stink of Dan's muffler disappeared. "Shit. Turn around."

"What?" Celia slowed and glanced around. I jumped out and doubled back down the road before the car stopped. "Bren! Bren! What's wrong?"

My heart pounded fast in my chest. I inhaled, thinking I'd lost the trail completely and raced further down the hill. I caught onto the weakening odor until it became more intense—telling my wolf I was headed in the right direction. The squealing tires and revving engine behind me told me Celia had turned the car around. I raced back, meeting her halfway. "Go back down the hill. They've taken Dan into the woods."

"Are you sure? We didn't pass anything even remotely resembling a road."

"I'm positive. The smell of exhaust cleared out." I frowned. "Didn't you notice?"

She gunned it. "I haven't scented anything since we left the club. How are you picking up anything with all the decomposing foliage around?"

"Tracking's the one thing I was always good at, Ceel—*Stop!*" I pointed to a break in the trees blanketed with ferns. "Right there."

Celia made a hard left and stomped on the accelerator to push the sedan up the small incline. She swore as the Lexus tore over drying wood and something hard slammed beneath the undercarriage.

I threw open the car door when the wheels spun. "We're making noise, babe. Come on. We go on foot from here."

Celia rushed out. "Maybe you should howl, and *call* the pack."

"And give away our location to these ghouls?" I shook my head. "They'll take it out on Dan and kill him for sure."

Celia started to say something, then nodded reluctantly. "I guess you're right."

We abandoned the path and jetted through the thickening forest with me leading the way. We might have hit the three mile mark when the air charged with the aroma of crushed herbs. Magic . . . more specifically, *witch* magic. I bit back a snarl, knowing we'd found the idiot forcing the spirits to rise.

We slowed to a stop. Celia crouched beside me and stole a wary glance, her tigress eyes replacing her own and taking in the darkness. "This is where the dead are being raised," her husky voice murmured. "I can smell the witch. She's near."

"Yeah, I know. Problem is, she knows we're here, too." I scanned the area, sensing the magic build like a small wave. "We must've triggered some kind of alarm."

The cold breeze stilled and the air crackled as if electrified the further we advanced into the dark forest. Celia nudged me and motioned to the sky. Dark clouds condensed like billowing smoke, swallowing the moon and the scattered stars littering the hemisphere. In a slasher flick, we'd be slated for our dooms and an audience full of movie-goers would be screaming at us to snag some garlic, a crucifix, find the nearest church, or just plain run. The slasher himself was about to break through the trees and get us.

Maybe. But let him try. No way was I ditching Dan.

Our beasts moved us like shadows, becoming one with

the forest and blending us into the encroaching darkness. My coursing blood pounded hard in my ears. Dan's scent of blood and fear intensified, inciting my beast to growl. He was still alive, and hurt.

Celia must have scented my increasing rage, and urged me to go faster. We leapt across a small brook where Dan's paisley hanky was left abandoned on the other side. I bent to lift it when the air charged once more.

Tarragon filtered through my nose and made me sneeze, cutting off my building snarls. Mist trailed from the rows of sweeping firs, cloaking the forest floor and edging its way across the thick ferns like a giant tarp. The hair on my body stood on end and my eyes caught view of Celia's blanching face. She knew what the mist possessed.

I just hoped it wouldn't possess us.

My head turned slow enough that I felt my tendons and muscles slide beneath my skin. Silver trickles of light illuminated from the ground, gradually lengthening until they formed into legs, torsos, arms, heads. Bodies of dead men and women. Pale versions of their former selves. Spirits.

"Oh, Jesus. Sweet Jesus," Celia whispered.

Cold sweat trickled down my spine while *The Exorcist*, *Poltergeist*, and every damn movie dealing with possession flashed through my mind in goddamn blue-ray, director's cut glory. I swore when they circled us, not sure how to get us out of this. Aric was right, I'd rushed in too quickly. And I'd fucking dragged his mate in with me.

Celia startled when I gripped her arm. It was my way of assuring her that I'd protect her with my life. Thing of it was, that didn't mean I'd manage to save hers. She trembled beneath my hold, or perhaps it was me doing the shaking. This shit was seriously messed up.

At least a dozen transparent bodies closed in around us. I stilled as the sudden whiff of their pain cut through the rapidly freezing air. My building panic faded and retreated deep into my core . . . and an odd sense of peace washed over me like a soothing shower. "They're not going to hurt us, Ceel." I didn't know how I knew. I just did. My wolf had risen to his feet within me, alert, but not in furious defense of hungry spooks about to devour our souls.

Something beckoned me to turn around. The spirit of a young woman, maybe twenty-five or so, with long, dark hair approached us, carrying a small bundle. Her expression held the grimness of someone who experienced a rough life and an even more wretched death. I didn't want her to show me what she clutched so caringly in her arms. I clenched my jaw harder and harder with every step she took until I thought I'd snap it from the tension.

She was a lot smaller than me. Her small bundle rested inches from my stomach. I wanted to grab Celia and bolt past her, except the spirit begged me without words not to turn away. She wanted me to see, to *feel*, in a way her suffering would no longer allow. Slowly, she unwrapped the faded gray blanket, likely light blue when it had mattered. I expected to find something out of my most ghoulish nightmares—a hideous face, disfigured, amputated, or equally scary as hell. It wasn't. In her arms lay a baby, nuzzling close to his mother's chest. Thick lashes grazed his chubby cheeks. Tiny lips pursed together. And a dimple dabbed his small perfect chin. He was . . . cute.

Was cute.

He opened his large eyes, blinking away sleep.

The mother raised him to me, insisting I hold him. But that was no longer possible. He was dead.

And so was she.

Celia leaned over the baby, smiling as best she could. Tears ran thick in her voice. "Your son is precious."

The ghost smiled and nodded while her cheeks were streaked with her pain.

To our right, the ghost of a young soldier smiled and waved. He shuffled forward, walking with an unsteady limp and dressed in a tattered WWII army uniform. I swore again, taking in the growing numbers rising from the mist. The spirits the witch had raised tonight had had their fill throughout the years. Their victims—men, women, and hell, even *babies* had suffered brutally at the hands of these assholes.

Celia's fury flared with mine. I placed my hand on her lower back and urged her forward. "We gotta get rid of the evil spirits and kill the bitch who raised them." I jerked my head back toward the woman and her baby. "It's the only way they'll get their peace."

The ghosts before us nodded with approval and parted, allowing us through. Rows of arms pointed in the direction of a steep ravine. Our pace quickened. A little boy of about six hurried beside us, trying to show Celia his small Matchbox truck. He wanted her to take it, but of course, it was no longer possible.

Celia swallowed hard when she tried to pat his head and her hand went right through him. "When we reach them, I'm taking out the witch. You go after Dan." She froze as we took in the brambles of dying blackberry bushes layering the ravine and the cold breeze shot upward. "I can smell Danny," she whispered.

The growl I'd forced back burned my throat. "Yeah, he's near. Stay close to me until we absolutely have to separate." I linked my fingers around hers. "Can you *shift* us down through these thorns?"

She nodded. "Hang tight."

We leapt high into the ravine. I barely caught sight of another spread of forest before ramming my eyes shut and holding my breath. Traveling via Celia left you with eyeballs and a stomach full of dirt if you didn't take the necessary precautions. My body jerked forward, pulled along by the sheer strength of Celia's power. We resurfaced in the patch of woods just as an explosion of blinding light and the roar of breaking wood thundered above us.

I shoved Celia out of the way half a second before she was struck by the giant fir breaking through a sea of dense branches. She landed atop a thick bed of moss unharmed. What sucked was I didn't move fast enough. The giant trunk slammed into me, pinning me to the forest floor and mashing in my chest.

Broken ribs punctured my lungs like knives. I howled from the burn, struggling to breathe. All I managed were a few gasps and a shitload of wheezes. Warm blood pooled somewhere beneath me while searing pain ravaged my chest and catapulted out into my collapsing limbs. *Mother's ass*, even my tongue hurt.

Celia scrambled to me, her expression blanching with fear. She pushed at the trunk. It wouldn't budge. She knelt beside me, searching my body for signs of life. She gasped when I blinked back at her. "Oh, my God. Bren, are you okay?"

I reached out a weak hand and touched the soft skin of her beautiful face. "I love you, Celia," I choked, struggling to speak. "I've always loved you."

Celia released an exasperated sigh and shook her head. "No you don't, Bren."

"Okay," I wheezed. "I don't. It just seemed like the right thing to say. Get this thing off me, will ya?"

Celia scanned the length of the trunk. "Okay, but I have to *change* to do it. Don't look while I take my clothes off."

She stood and immediately started stripping. My lids peeled opened over my head. Dan was in trouble, my lungs were hamburger, and I was pretty sure my liver had split in two. I still watched her. Closely. Don't judge me. Knocking on death's door or not, I was still a man, damn it.

Wow. Celia looks even hotter than the last time I saw her naked. I wonder if Aric ever—

"*Bren!* I told you not to look!"

I frowned. "I never agreed to that."

She *changed*, unleashing the golden tigress eager to kick ass. Her front claws dug into the bark while her back claws pushed against the forest floor. I roared as the weight rolled off me. It would've landed on my right arm if Celia hadn't managed to hurl it at the last moment.

She nudged me with her large furry face, helping me to sit when I continued to writhe on the frozen ground like a salted slug. My crushed ribs withdrew from my lungs and slid beneath my skin to realign against my sternum. A barrage of swears spat out my mouth. *Holy Mother*, it hurt. The pain skyrocketed into mind-blinding agony when my ribs snapped back into place one after the other.

My vision blurred, and for a moment I came close to blacking out. But it didn't matter. I'd heal. But Celia wasn't *were*. She didn't have the ability to mend her wounds. *Son of a whore*. That tree would've killed her if it had landed on her. But I guessed that's what the shit-witch who aimed it at us wanted.

It took me another few breaths to rise. When I finally stumbled to my feet, it was Celia's turn to save my ass. She shoved me back behind the fallen tree just as a funnel of green and red raged toward us, burning a path through the forest like the mother of all infernos.

Flames engulfed the longer branches of our cover, barbequing the air above our heads. *Holy shit.* We'd just missed getting burned to bacon. As the flames died down, we cautiously peered over the trunk, following the path seared by the fire.

Across the long stretch of burning embers, a woman with long pale hair and a black velvet dress stood holding a staff loosely against her side and smiling. Her smile faded when Celia stood and licked her chops.

I patted Celia's furry side. "Okay, little pussy. There's your mouse."

The witch gripped her staff and pointed it at Celia when she charged, chanting in frightened spurts, building her magic.

Streams of green and red shot from her staff as Celia bounded toward her. But my girl was too damn quick. Her tigress form jumped and swerved with lightning speed, avoiding the flames as if they were nothing more than twirling ribbons. She *shifted* when she was mere yards away, and appeared in a high leap. The witch lifted her staff and surrounded herself with a protection bubble, just barely missing getting pounced and clawed. She screamed when Celia slammed into her magical shield and cracked it with just one blow. The bubble splintered, obstructing the witch's terrified face.

That eerie feeling returned as I watched, raising the hairs on my neck like flags. Once again a dense mist overtook the land. The temperature dropped . . . and the tormented ghosts rose from the ground. They gathered slowly around Celia and the witch, their numbers building—watching, waiting for Celia to break through. The way she pounded her massive claws against the protective shield, she'd soon reach her prey. Celia would make sure this Tribe tramp would never raise evil spirits again.

And I'd make sure to send the asswipes back to hell.

I fought my way to my feet, while agony continued to tear its way through my body like bubbling acid. I howled, both from the struggle to rise and to *call* the pack. Pricks or not, I needed them here.

From a very, very, *very*, long distance away, another wolf answered my *call*.

For shit's sake. It's going to take them forever to get here.

My head snapped up at the sound of Dan's pained screams. *Jesus.* They'd started eating his soul. I hobbled toward his growing cries, my pain making me annoyingly slow. I swore, still unable to catch my breath. With a grunt and another few more creative swears, I forced my legs to move faster, biting through the pain and stumbling over every damn rock, log, and creeping vine.

I reached a clearing, staggering to a halt at the sight of a cluster of naked blue and brown women piled on top of each other, clawing, hissing, and fighting over what lay beneath them. Their heads jerked up as my growls built into a hateful roar.

They growled in challenge, their beauty gone, replaced by shriveled, sagging skin, and sunken faces that bared their thirst and hunger. One by one they slithered out of their pile, flashing their pointy teeth and wicked claws. I advanced, only fifty yards remained between me and them. I was going to kill them and then find Dan. They would pay for hurting him. . . .

I didn't see Dan until the last of the *Ciguapas* lifted from his unmoving form. His head lay twisted in an odd angle and blood smeared the lapels of his polyester suit.

They'd killed him. They'd killed my best friend.

Something fired deep within me, a trigger for the rage I'd always kept carefully in check. But there was no need to slap the safety on now. I buried the torturous pain of my mending and exploded with fury, *changing* into my wolf form and surrendering to a beast whose need for carnage knew no end.

They'd murdered my friend, my brother, my family, my *pack*, and now these fuckers were going to pay!

My claws dug into the frozen earth, kicking it behind me as I sped forward. The *Ciguapas* spread out. They refused to go to hell without a fight.

But they had no goddamn clue who they were fighting.

A long-forgotten scent from my past stopped my onslaught like a whip strangling my neck. My eyes widened as I ground to a halt. My body tumbled and rolled from the force of my sudden stop, lashing at and aggravating my injuries. But the pain was secondary to the rush of emotions I felt then. I scrambled to my feet, my throat tightening into a hard knot that threatened to choke me.

Shit.

Before me stood my human mother, her arms outstretched and her face breaking into that familiar look of love she'd always greeted me with.

I shook my giant head, trying to clear my vision. *This isn't happening.* I blinked my eyes open, convinced she'd vanished. But there she stood, smiling patiently. I inched forward, wanting and needing to believe it was her. My father had killed them both when he tried to *turn* her werewolf, I reminded myself. He'd failed, I insisted. They weren't coming back.

And still there she was.

She strode toward me, moving in her signature determined walk, her dark curly hair bouncing against her shoulders. *"Bren,"* she said quietly, speaking in that same melodious tone I remembered and struggled to forget. "My son!"

Without fear, she knelt and embraced my wide neck, her aroma of sunflowers claiming it was undeniably her. She smiled softly and stroked my head, just like she had when I was a scared little boy. "Everything is going to be all right. I promise, Bren."

That's when I tore out her goddamn throat.

The body that crumbled at my feet was not my mother. I was positive even before she morphed back to one of those goddamn ghosts. My mother *never* promised shit. Even when I begged her to tell me she and dad would survive the *turn*. That should've been my first damn clue they would die.

The taste of her blood riled my wolf and made him crave more. My hind legs launched me forward, throwing me into several of the remaining freaks at once. They fought like rabid animals, raking my back, limbs, and face with their sharp nails and piercing my flesh with their fangs.

It did jack against my beast.

I tasted their fear as it spilled down my jowls in pools of gray blood. I wanted them to suffer. And I wanted them to convulse in misery for what they'd done to Dan.

Dan had never hurt anyone. He was kind and smart and loyal. He was the first person I ever told about my pathetic past.

I thought he'd pity me. Instead that beanpole looked me in the eye and told me he was proud of me for surviving without parents, a pack, and a dime to my name. He had the purest heart of any man in this goddamn world and now he was gone.

My claws cracked open chests, my fangs severed necks. *Fuck you for taking him away from me, from Celia, from her sisters, from the world. Fuck you!*

"Bren, leave them . . . They're dead, Bren, they're dead."

Celia's pained voice tore me away from the chunks of gray flesh my fangs continued to shred and gnaw. She knelt over Dan in her human form, pushing down on his chest and filling his lungs with her breath. Tears streaked her bloody face as she sobbed and pleaded him not to die.

My body lurched forward and bound to their side. Dan's vacant and unblinking stare was like a punch in the gut. My wolf eyes took in his chalk white skin and blue lips, while the man within me begged him to move, to speak, to *breathe*.

I sniffed at him. . . . Christ, he was still alive, but my wolf could sense the light in his soul dwindling away with every passing moment. Every muscle in my body tensed. I couldn't let him die. He needed a chance.

I shoved Celia away and pierced his heart with my fangs.

I vaguely remember her screaming and trying to wrench me off him before the world faded into black.

Chapter Eight

Sunlight beat against my heavy lids, determined it was time to wake my ass up. I blinked several times, fighting the haze that followed one hell of a nap. I swore and rubbed my eyes. Damn, I was friggin' starving. The warm sheet slipped from my chest, exposing my pecs as I pushed up on my elbows and took in my bedroom at a glance. Hell, someone had tidied up. A basket full of clean laundry lay folded on top of my bureau, filling my nose with the clean scent of "summer breeze" fabric softener. And shit, had the babe lying next to me vacuumed?

I did a double-take when I realized the "babe" sleeping beside me was Celia. She cuddled against my pillow and tucked her bare feet deeper beneath her long brown skirt, causing the collar of her light blue sweater to droop between the swells of her breasts. I yanked her by the waist and pulled her to me, burying my nose into her neck. "I always knew we'd end up in bed."

She laughed and pushed me off of her, smiling as she wiped the sleep from her eyes. "I see you're finally awake, sleeping beauty." Her smile softened as she sat up. "Do you feel okay?"

"Yeah, I guess." I scratched at my beard, pausing when I realized how thick it was. "How long have I been out?"

Celia reached for her cell phone. "Hmm, almost forty hours. You missed a full moon last night."

I jerked up as a swarm of memories came flooding back. The spirits . . . the witch . . . Shit—*Dan!*

Celia cupped my shoulder gently with her small hand and smiled. "He's okay, Bren. You did it." She glanced at the door when the soft pads of urgent feet echoed down the hall. "Speaking of which . . ."

A giant wolf stumbled in his haste to round the corner and launched himself upward. He landed in a belly flop between us before scrambling to the foot of the bed. Jesus, never had I seen such an ungainly lupine.

The wolf spread out his long scrawny body. An excited glimmer lightened his intelligent amber eyes while his long tongue draped out of his mouth in true goofball glory. "Dan?" He wagged his tail and barked out a happy yip. "You're . . . fucking *blue*."

Celia laughed again and leaned forward to stroke the top of his narrow head. "He's a blue merle, extremely rare for a werewolf. According to the pack Elders it's symbolic of rare and powerful magic." A note of concern shadowed her husky voice. "He's supposed to develop a special ability. One that will impact the entire *were* race." She cleared her throat and forced a hopeful smile. "He keeps admiring himself in the mirror and hasn't wanted to *change* back to human." Her smile widened, becoming more genuine. "I must say, he is awfully cute."

Dan's tail thumped louder against the mattress. He jerked up suddenly and dive-bombed Celia with his ridiculously dorky tongue. Celia wrinkled her nose and batted his long snout. "Ew, Danny. Cut it out."

Dan was alive, well, and a goddamn blue werewolf. Maybe knowing his freak new *were* mo-jo could knock our entire species on its ass should've scared me, but it didn't—at least not then. I was stoked we'd survived and decided it was time my boy had some fun.

I locked Celia in a full nelson and hooked my legs around hers. "Get her, Dan! Get her! Come on, fella!"

Dan was on Celia like duct tape, slathering her face with his werewolf love. Celia squirmed and squealed. "Don't. . . . Stop. . . . Knock it off. . . . *Ew*!"

"I believe she asked you to stop."

We froze at the sound of Aric's deep voice. He stood in the doorway, his arms crossed, his thick brows angling into a frown. Unlike Dan, the stealthy bastard hadn't made a sound.

I released Celia. She hurried to pull down her skirt. Oops. The hem had bunched up during the struggle and—oh *shit*—hiked all the way past her lacey pink panties.

Dan's tail curled between his legs, his submissive nature buckling in Aric's strong presence. "*Dan*," I warned, my jaw tightening. "If you piss on my bed, I'm going to beat your ass with a newspaper."

Aric's brows softened when he locked eyes with Celia, his eyes sparking with heat and tenderness completely unfamiliar to me. Celia's lips parted and her irises sizzled, giving him back what she'd sensed in his stare. She wiped her face on her sleeve, her cheeks warming to a soft blush. "Hi, Aric," she murmured.

"Hello, Celia."

They stared at each other, forgetting the rest of us. No one made a sound. And except for Dan's ears drooping, no one made a move, either. I let Celia and Aric have their moment, but it was a hell of a long moment. Just when I was about to yell at them to get their own damn room, Celia dropped her gaze and slipped to the edge of bed.

She tugged on her slouchy suede boots. "I should go."

Aric's expression hardened, the angles of his face tightening with frustration and annoyance. *Now, that's a look I knew oh so well.*

He huffed. "I guess you wouldn't want to keep *Misha* waiting."

Oh, shit.

"And I'll just bet your *fiancée* can't wait to have you back," she snapped.

I tucked my hands behind my head. "Actually, Ceel, I doubt that angry bitch is at the edge of her seat waiting for Aric." She glanced at me over her shoulder. "You see, I kinda let her read his note."

Celia's eyes widened and she cleared her throat, trying to squelch her expanding grin. It didn't work. Aric caught it and lowered his head. She shoved her cell phone in her purse and walked toward the door, slowing as she neared and pausing beside him.

Aric maintained his position against the frame, casually leaning back with his arms folded over his chest. His nose flared slightly, capturing her scent. Like a shy teen, Celia played with the strap of her purse as she spoke to him. "I'm sorry I didn't listen to you when you told me not to go after Danny. I wasn't trying to pick a fight or insult you. I just wanted to help our friend."

Aric hooked a long strand of her hair with his finger and tucked it behind her ear then slowly trailed his finger across her jaw line, using it to lift her chin. "It's not that I didn't think you could help. I know you're tough. But you were facing an enemy that could have robbed you of your soul." He released her then but kept his eyes trained on her. "It would destroy me if anything ever happened to you."

For a moment, I was sure Celia was going to say something back—maybe about his declaration of their matehood in the letter. But she instead she averted her gaze and walked away . . . even though he continued to watch her closely.

"Quit staring at her ass," I yelled when his eyes trailed her out of the room.

"Don't be an asshole, Bren," she hissed from the end of the hall.

"He's the one eyeing your butt cheeks like they can fold paper," I shot back defensively.

The door slammed, cutting off Celia's growl. Aric rubbed his face, trying to beat back the heat crawling up his neck. "Thanks, *Bren*."

I scratched Dan's ears, my grin widening. "No problem, boss. So, to what do we owe the pleasure?"

"I came to speak with you about what happened the other night. You should have howled a *call* the moment those spirits showed up."

"Why? Because Celia was with me?"

Aric paused. "In part, but also because you were in danger, and so were the humans we're sworn to protect."

"Nah. You would've been too distracted trying to get Celia alone so you could make out with her." Aric stared at me, probably torn between snapping my neck and laughing. Either way, the prick didn't deny it.

He cleared his throat, struggling it seemed, to wrangle in his patience. Hmm. Wonder why?

"Your pack is not your enemy, Bren. You have to stop perceiving us as such."

I opened my mouth, ready to make some wiseass remark. But considering I dragged my tail into danger and took Celia along for the ride, I knew the bastard had a point. I'd needed them and had waited too damn long to *call* in our location.

Aric watched me, his expression stern. "I hate to admit it, but you did a hell of a job tracking Dan. I don't know if another *were* could have fixed on such a weak trail."

"So?"

A smirk cut through his serious demeanor. "So, I think I found the perfect forum for your skills."

I rolled my eyes. "You want me to teach the little pukes at the Den how to track, don't you?"

Aric grinned. "Damn, Bren. It's like you can read my mind—just no sex talk. Stick to the subject and you won't piss me off."

"Okay, if I must. But what if one of the little bastards has a question about getting laid?"

"Then you can direct him to me."

"Shouldn't I direct him to someone who's actually getting some?"

Aric pinched the bridge of his nose and growled something about me being a monstrous pain in the ass. He pushed off the doorframe to leave, but I stopped him.

"Can I ask you something?"

At first, I thought I pissed him off enough to say no. But then he crossed his arms again and gave me a stiff nod. "Go ahead."

"My dad failed to *turn* my mother wolf. How the hell did I manage to *turn* Dan?"

Aric abandoned the doorway and lowered himself into the old beat-up leather chair by my bed. He leaned forward, resting his arms on his thighs. "Bren, the *turning* process is complex; it's not just about piercing another's heart and transferring your wolf's essence. If it were, we'd have more *weres*. The Elders believe the donors and recipients have to be spiritually and physically tough to endure one soul's invasion of another's." He shook his head. "Even then, if their love for each other is weak, they'll fail."

I growled defensively. "You sayin' my parents' love wasn't strong? You don't know shit. They were mates, goddamn you!"

I should have known better than to challenge an Alpha, especially one who'd already whooped my ass. And yet for some reason, Aric didn't respond with aggression.

His shoulders remained relaxed and he continued, dismissing the growls that continued to burn a hole in my gut. "I told you what the Elders believe. What I didn't explain was that a lot can go wrong. Your father could have released your mother too soon, or his fangs may not have punctured her heart deep enough. I didn't know your father. But I know it killed him to cause his mate pain." He lowered his head and stared at his palms. "If he didn't commit to the task out of fear of hurting her, he failed her even before he began."

I took in the sadness creasing the edges of his eyes. "Are we still talking about my folks?" I asked like a dumb-ass.

Aric paused, then slowly leaned back. He ignored my question and glanced between me and Dan. "I think it helped that Dan was dying. Your desperation to save him committed you to *turning* him. Under other circumstances, I can't be sure you would've survived."

I paused to think about what Aric said. "I guess that makes sense. Here's the thing, though, most successful *turns* occur between mated couples—or those who love each other deeply."

Aric nodded. "That's right. Otherwise the human's soul would reject the *were's*."

"Well, boss, Dan and me aren't a couple. Does this mean he's been secretly in love with me this whole time? I mean, I can't blame him if he is, I'm pretty damn awesome—"

Dan actually growled at me. Aric rolled with laughter and it took him a moment to collect himself. "The *turning* process is typically done between mated couples because their love is believed strong enough to survive the experience. But you're forgetting there are other kinds of love—like that between brothers, which you and Dan appear to share."

Dan wagged his tail when I turned to acknowledge him. I grinned and patted his back. "Okay. Thanks, Aric."

He stood to leave. "I'll expect you at the Den tomorrow, on time and ready to work."

"Yeah, yeah, I read the note, remember?"

Aric huffed. "Yes, and not only did you read it, but you passed it around like a damn hors d'oeuvre."

I chuckled. "I guess I shouldn't have shown it to Celia . . . or your fiancée."

Aric shrugged. "I don't care who saw it, everything in it is true."

My spine stiffened. "Even the part about Celia being your mate?"

"Yes, that, and the part where I call you a loser."

I barked out a laugh. "You don't care that what's-her-face got mad?"

His expression hardened, losing its humor. "No. I only care what Celia thinks."

"Well, she thought enough to ask to keep it."

My comment seemed to surprise him. "She did?"

"Yup, she'll probably sleep with it under her pillow."

Aric laughed and headed for the door. He stopped before walking out and glanced over his shoulder. "Thank you for keeping her safe."

I nodded but didn't respond. Celia was part of my pack—the real one. And packmates would take a cursed gold bullet for one of their own. My stomach growled as Aric disappeared, furious I'd gone so long without feeding it. I slapped Dan's skinny rump and nudged him out of bed. "Woman, you better put on that French maid outfit and fix me some grub. Daddy's hungry."

Read on as the Weird Girls saga continues with Sealed with a Curse, the first full length novel in The Weird Girls Urban Fantasy Romance series by Cecy Robson. The excerpt has been set for this edition only and may not reflect the final content of the final novel.

Sealed with a Curse

A Weird Girls Novel

By

CECY ROBSON

Chapter One

Sacramento, California

The courthouse doors crashed open as I led my three sisters into the large foyer. I didn't mean to push so hard, but hell, I was mad and worried about being eaten. The cool spring breeze slapped at my back as I stepped inside, yet it did little to cool my temper or my nerves.

My nose scented the vampires before my eyes caught them emerging from the shadows. There were six of them, wearing dark suits, Ray-Bans, and obnoxious little grins. Two bolted the doors tight behind us, while the others frisked us for weapons.

I can't believe we we're in vampire court. So much for avoiding the perilous world of the supernatural.

Emme trembled beside me. She had every right to be scared. We were strong, but our combined abilities couldn't trump a roomful of bloodsucking beasts. "Celia," she whispered, her voice shaking. "Maybe we shouldn't have come."

Like we had a choice. "Just stay close to me, Emme." My muscles tensed as the vampire's hands swept the length of my body and through my long curls. I didn't like him touching me, and neither did my inner tigress. My fingers itched with the need to protrude my claws.

When he finally released me, I stepped closer to Emme

while I scanned the foyer for a possible escape route. Next to me, the vampire searching Taran got a little daring with his pat-down. But he was messing with the wrong sister.

"If you touch my ass one more time, fang boy, I swear to God I'll light you on fire." The vampire quickly removed his hands when a spark of blue flame ignited from Taran's fingertips.

Shayna, conversely, flashed a lively smile when the vampire searching her found her toothpicks. Her grin widened when he returned her seemingly harmless little sticks, unaware of how deadly they were in her hands. "Thanks, dude." She shoved the box back into the pocket of her slacks.

"They're clear." The guard grinned at Emme and licked his lips. "This way." He motioned her to follow. Emme cowered. Taran showed no fear and plowed ahead. She tossed her dark, wavy hair and strutted into the courtroom like the diva she was, wearing a tiny white mini dress that contrasted with her deep olive skin. I didn't fail to notice the guards' gazes glued to Taran's shapely figure. Nor did I miss when their incisors lengthened, ready to bite.

I urged Emme and Shayna forward. "Go. I'll watch your backs." I whipped around to snarl at the guards. The vampires' smiles faltered when they saw *my* fangs protrude. Like most beings, they probably didn't know what I was, but they seemed to recognize that I was potentially lethal, despite my petite frame.

I followed my sisters into the large courtroom. The place reminded me of a picture I'd seen of the Salem witch trials. Rows of dark wood pews lined the center aisle, and wide rustic planks comprised the floor. Unlike the photo I recalled, every window was boarded shut, and paintings of vampires hung on every inch of available wall space. One particular image epitomized the vampire stereotype perfectly. It showed a male vampire entwined with two naked women on a bed of roses and jewels. The women appeared completely enamored of the vampire, even while blood dripped from their necks.

The vampire spectators scrutinized us as we approached along the center aisle. Many had accessorized their expensive attire with diamond jewelry and watches that probably cost more than my car. Their glares told me they didn't appreciate my cotton T-shirt, peasant skirt, and flip-flops. I was twenty-five years old; it's not like I didn't know how to dress. But, hell, other fabrics and shoes were way more expensive to replace when I *changed* into my other form.

I spotted our accuser as we stalked our way to the front of the assembly. Even in a courtroom crammed with young and sexy vampires, Misha Aleksandr stood out. His tall, muscular frame filled his fitted suit, and his long blond hair brushed against his shoulders. Death, it seemed, looked damn good. Yet it wasn't his height or his wealth or even his striking features that captivated me. He possessed a fierce presence that commanded the room. Misha Aleksandr was a force to be reckoned with, but, strangely enough, so was I.

Misha had "requested" our presence in Sacramento after charging us with the murder of one of his family members. We had two choices: appear in court or be hunted for the rest of our lives. The whole situation sucked. We'd stayed hidden from the supernatural world for so long. Now not only had we been forced into the limelight, but we also faced the possibility of dying some twisted, Rob Zombie–inspired death.

Of course, God forbid that would make Taran shut her trap. She leaned in close to me. "Celia, how about I gather some magic-borne sunlight and fry these assholes?" she whispered in Spanish.

A few of the vampires behind us muttered and hissed, causing uproar among the rest. If they didn't like us before, they sure as hell hated us then.

Shayna laughed nervously, but maintained her perky demeanor. "I think some of them understand the lingo, dude."

I recognized Taran's desire to burn the vamps to blood and ash, but I didn't agree with it. Conjuring such power would leave her drained and vulnerable, easy prey for the master vampires, who would be immune to her sunlight. Besides, we were already in trouble with one master for killing his keep. We didn't need to be hunted by the entire leeching species.

The procession halted in a strangely wide-open area before a raised dais. There were no chairs or tables, nothing we could use as weapons against the judges or the angry mob amassed behind us.

My eyes focused on one of the boarded windows. The light honey-colored wood frame didn't match the darker boards. I guessed the last defendant had tried to escape. Judging from the claw marks running from beneath the frame to where I stood, he, she, or *it* hadn't made it.

I looked up from the deeply scratched floor to find Misha's intense gaze on me. We locked eyes, predator to predator, neither of us the type to back down. *You're trying to intimidate the wrong gal, pretty boy. I don't scare easily.*

Shayna slapped her hand over her face and shook her head, her long black ponytail waving behind her. "For Pete's sake, Celia, can't you be a little friendlier?" She flashed Misha a grin that made her blue eyes sparkle. "How's it going, dude?"

Shayna said "dude" a lot, ever since dating some idiot claiming to be a professional surfer. The term fit her sunny personality and eventually grew on us.

Misha didn't appear taken by her charm. He eyed her as if she'd asked him to make her a garlic pizza in the shape of a cross. I laughed; I couldn't help it. *Leave it to Shayna to try to befriend the guy who'll probably suck us dry by sundown.*

At the sound of my chuckle, Misha regarded me slowly. His head tilted slightly as his full lips curved into a sensual smile. I would have preferred a vicious stare—I knew how to deal with those. For a moment, I thought he'd somehow made my clothes disappear and I was standing there like the bleeding hoochies in that awful painting.

The judges' sudden arrival gave me an excuse to glance away. There were four, each wearing a formal robe of red velvet with an elaborate powdered wig. They were probably several centuries old, but like all vampires, they didn't appear a day over thirty. Their splendor easily surpassed the beauty of any mere mortal. I guessed the whole "sucky, sucky, me love you all night" lifestyle paid off for them.

The judges regally assumed their places on the raised dais. Behind them hung a giant plasma screen, which appeared out of place in this century-old building. Did they plan to watch a movie while they decided how best to disembowel us?

A female judge motioned Misha forward with a Queen Elizabeth hand wave. A long, thick scar angled from the corner of her left jaw across her throat. Someone had tried to behead her. To scar a vampire like that, the culprit had likely used a gold blade reinforced with lethal magic. Apparently, even that blade hadn't been enough. I gathered she commanded the fang-fest Parliament, since her marble nameplate read, CHIEF JUSTICE ANTOINETTE MALIKA. Judge Malika didn't strike me as the warm and cuddly sort. Her lips were pursed into a tight line and her elongating fangs locked over her lower lip. I only hoped she'd snacked before her arrival.

At a nod from Judge Malika, Misha began. "Members of the High Court, I thank you for your audience." A Russian accent underscored his deep voice. "I hereby charge Celia, Taran, Shayna, and Emme Wird with the murder of my family member, David Geller."

"Wird? More like *Weird*," a vamp in the audience mumbled. The smaller vamp next to him adjusted his bow tie nervously when I snarled.

Oh, yeah, like we've never heard that before, jerk.

The sole male judge slapped a heavy leather-bound book on the long table and whipped out a feather quill. "Celia Wird. State your position."

Position?

I exchanged glances with my sisters; they didn't seem to know what Captain Pointy Teeth meant either. Taran shrugged. "Who gives a shit? Just say something."

I waved a hand. "Um. Registered nurse?"

Judging by his "please don't make me eat you before the proceedings" scowl, and the snickering behind us, I hadn't provided him with the appropriate response.

He enunciated every word carefully and slowly so as to not further confuse my obviously feeble and inferior mind. "Position in the supernatural world."

"We've tried to avoid your world." I gave Taran the evil eye. "For the most part. But if you must know, I'm a tigress."

"Weretigress," he said as he wrote.

"I'm not a *were*," I interjected defensively.

He huffed. "Can you *change* into a tigress or not?"

"Well, yes. But that doesn't make me a *were*."

The vamps behind us buzzed with feverish whispers while

the judges' eyes narrowed suspiciously. Not knowing what we were made them nervous. A nervous vamp was a dangerous vamp. And the room was bursting with them.

"What I mean is, unlike a *were*, I can *change* parts of my body without turning into my beast completely." And unlike anything else on earth, I could also *shift*—disappear under and across solid ground and resurface unscathed. But they didn't need to know that little tidbit. Nor did they need to know I couldn't heal my injuries. If it weren't for Emme's unique ability to heal herself and others, my sisters and I would have died long ago.

"Fascinating," he said in a way that clearly meant I wasn't. The feather quill didn't come with an eraser. And the judge obviously didn't appreciate my making him mess up his book. He dipped his pen into his little inkwell and scribbled out what he'd just written before addressing Taran. "Taran Wird, position?"

"I can release magic into the forms of fire and lightning—"

"Very well, witch." The vamp scrawled.

"I'm not a witch, asshole."

The judge threw his plume on the table, agitated. Judge Malika fixed her frown on Taran. "What did you say?"

Nobody flashed a vixen grin better than Taran. "I said, 'I'm not a witch. Ass. Hole.'"

Emme whimpered, ready to hurl from the stress. Shayna giggled and threw an arm around Taran. "She's just kidding, dude!"

No. Taran didn't kid. Hell, she didn't even know any knock-knock jokes. She shrugged off Shayna, unwilling to back down. She wouldn't listen to Shayna. But she would listen to me.

"Just answer the question, Taran."

The muscles on Taran's jaw tightened, but she did as I asked. "I make fire, light—"

"Fire-breather." Captain Personality wrote quickly.

"I'm not a—"

He cut her off. "Shayna Wird?"

"Well, dude, I throw knives—"

"Knife thrower," he said, ready to get this little meet-and-greet over and done with.

Shayna did throw knives. That was true. She could also transform pieces of wood into razor-sharp weapons and manipulate alloys. All she needed was metal somewhere on her body and a little focus. For her safety, though, "knife thrower" seemed less threatening.

"And you, Emme Wird?"

"Um. Ah. I can move things with my mind—"

"Gypsy," the half-wit interpreted.

I supposed "telekinetic" was too big a word for this idiot. Then again, unlike typical telekinetics, Emme could do more than bend a few forks. I sighed. *Tigress, fire-breather, knife thrower, and Gypsy.* We sounded like the headliners for a freak show. All we needed was a bearded lady. I sighed. *That's what happens when you're the bizarre products of a back-fired curse.*

Misha glanced at us quickly before stepping forward once more. "I will present Mr. Hank Miller and Mr. Timothy Brown as witnesses—" Taran exhaled dramatically and twirled her hair like she was bored. Misha glared at her before finishing. "I do not doubt justice will be served."

Judge Zhahara Nadim, who resembled more of an Egyptian queen than someone who should be stuffed into a powdered wig, surprised me by leering at Misha like she wanted his head for a lawn ornament. I didn't know what he'd done to piss her off; yet knowing we weren't the only ones hated brought me a strange sense of comfort. She narrowed her eyes at Misha, like all predators do before they strike, and called forward someone named "Destiny." I didn't know Destiny, but I knew she was no vampire the moment she strutted onto the dais.

I tried to remain impassive. However, I really wanted to run away screaming. Short of sporting a few tails and some extra digits, Destiny was the freakiest thing I'd ever seen. Not only did she lack the allure all vampires possessed, but her fashion sense bordered on disastrous. She wore black patterned tights, white strappy sandals, and a hideous black-and-white polka-dot turtleneck. I guessed she sought to draw attention from her lime green zebra-print miniskirt. And, my God, her makeup was abominable. Black kohl outlined her bright fuchsia lips, and mint green shadow ringed her eyes.

"This is a perfect example of why I don't wear makeup," I

told Taran.

Taran stepped forward with her hands on her hips. "How the hell is *she* a witness? I didn't see her at the club that night! And Lord knows she would've stuck out."

Emme trembled beside me. "Taran, please don't get us killed!"

I gave my youngest sister's hand a squeeze. "Steady, Emme."

Judge Malika called Misha's two witnesses forward. "Mr. Miller and Mr. Brown, which of you gentlemen would like to go first?"

Both "gentlemen" took one gander at Destiny and scrambled away from her. It was never a good sign when something scared a vampire. Hank, the bigger of the two vamps, shoved Tim forward.

"You may begin," Judge Malika commanded. "Just concentrate on what you saw that night. Destiny?"

The four judges swiftly donned protective earwear, like construction workers used, just as a guard flipped a switch next to the flat-screen. At first, I thought the judges toyed with us. Even with heightened senses, how could they hear the testimony through those ridiculous ear guards? Before I could protest, Destiny enthusiastically approached Tim and grabbed his head. Tim's immediate bloodcurdling screams caused the rest of us to cover our ears. Every hair on my body stood at attention. What freaked me out was that he wasn't the one on trial.

Emme's fair freckled skin blanched so severely, I feared she'd pass out. Shayna stood frozen with her jaw open while Taran and I exchanged "oh, shit" glances. I was about to start the "let's get the hell out of here" ball rolling when images from Tim's mind appeared on the screen. I couldn't believe my eyes. Complete with sound effects, we relived the night of David's murder. Misha straightened when he saw David soar out of Taran's window in flames, but otherwise he did not react. Nor did Misha blink when what remained of David burst into ashes on our lawn. Still, I sensed his fury. The image moved to a close-up of Hank's shocked face and finished with the four of us scowling down at the blood and ash.

Destiny abruptly released the sobbing Tim, who collapsed

on the floor. Mucus oozed from his nose and mouth. I didn't even know vamps were capable of such body fluids.

At last, Taran finally seemed to understand the deep shittiness of our situation. "Son of a bitch," she whispered.

Hank gawked at Tim before addressing the judges. "If it pleases the court, I swear on my honor I witnessed exactly what Tim Brown did about David Geller's murder. My version would be of no further benefit."

Malika shrugged indifferently. "Very well, you're excused." She turned toward us while Hank hurried back to his seat. "As you just saw, we have ways to expose the truth. Destiny is able to extract memories, but she cannot alter them. Likewise, during Destiny's time with you, you will be unable to change what you saw. You'll only review what has already come to pass."

I frowned. "How do we know you're telling us the truth?" Malika peered down her nose at me. "What choice do you have? Now, which of you is first?"

Reader's Guide to the Magical World

of the Weird Girls Series

acute bloodlust A condition that occurs when a vampire goes too long without consuming blood. Increases the vampire's thirst to lethal levels. It is remedied by feeding the vampire.

Call The ability of one supernatural creature to reach out to another, through either thoughts or sounds. A vampire can pass his or her *call* by transferring a bit of magic into the receiving being's skin.

Change To transform from one being to another, typically from human to beast, and back again.

chronic bloodlust A condition caused by a curse placed on a vampire. It makes the vampire's thirst for blood insatiable and drives the vampire to insanity. The vampire grows in size from gluttony and assumes deformed features. There is no cure.

claim The method by which a werebeast consummates the union with his or her mate.

clan A group of werebeasts led by an Alpha. The types of clans differ depending on species. Werewolf clans are called "packs." Werelions belong to "prides."

Creatura The offspring of a demon lord and a werebeast.

dantem animam A soul giver. A rare being capable of returning a master vampire's soul. A master with a soul is more powerful than any other vampire in existence, as he or she is balancing life and death at once.

dark ones Creatures considered to be pure evil, such as shape-shifters or demons.

demon A creature residing in hell. Only the strongest demons may leave to stalk on earth, but their time is limited; the power of good compels them to return.

demon child The spawn of a demon lord and a mortal female. Demon children are of limited intelligence and rely predominantly on their predatory instincts.

demon lords (*demonkin*) The offspring of a witch mother and a demon. Powerful, cunning, and deadly. Unlike demons, whose time on earth is limited, demon lords may remain on earth indefinitely.

den A school where young werebeasts train and learn to fight in order to help protect the earth from mystical evil.

Elder One of the governors of a werebeast clan. Each clan is led by three Elders: an Alpha, a Beta, and an Omega. The Alpha is the supreme leader. The Beta is the second in command. The Omega settles disputes between them and has the ability to calm by releasing bits of his or her harmonized soul, or through a sense of humor muddled with magic. He possesses rare gifts and is often volatile, selfish, and of questionable loyalty.

force Emme Wird's ability to move objects with her mind.

gold The metallic element; it was cursed long ago and has damaging effects on werebeasts, vampires, and the dark ones. Supernatural creatures cannot hold gold without feeling the poisonous effects of the curse. A bullet dipped in gold will explode a supernatural creature's heart like a bomb. Gold against open skin has a searing effect.

grandmaster The master of a master vampire. Grandmasters are among the earth's most powerful creatures. Grandmasters can recognize whether the human he or she *turned* is a master upon creation. Grandmasters usually kill any master vampires they create to consume their power. Some choose to let the masters live until they become a threat, or until they've gained greater strength and therefore more consumable power.

Hag Hags, like witches, are born with their magic. They have a tendency for mischief and are as infamous for their instability as they are their power.

keep Beings a master vampire controls and is responsible for, such as those he or she has *turned* vampire, or a human he or she regularly feeds from. One master can acquire another's keep by destroying the master the keep belongs to.

Leader A pureblood werebeast in charge of delegating and planning attacks against the evils that threaten the earth.

Lesser witch Title given to a witch of weak power and who has not yet mastered control of her magic. Unlike their Superior counterparts, they aren't given talismans or staffs to amplify their magic because their control over their power is limited.

Lone A werebeast who doesn't belong to a clan, and therefore is not obligated to protect the earth from supernatural evil. Considered of lower class by those with clans.

master vampire A vampire with the ability to *turn* a human vampire. Upon their creation, masters are usually killed by their grandmaster for power. Masters are immune to fire and to sunlight born of magic, and typically carry tremendous power. Only a master or another lethal preternatural can kill a master vampire. If one master kills another, the surviving vampire acquires his or her power, wealth, and keep.

mate The being a werebeast will love and share a soul with for eternity.

Misericordia A plea for mercy in a duel.

moon sickness The werebeast equivalent of bloodlust. Brought on by a curse from a powerful enchantress. Causes excruciating pain. Attacks a werebeast's central nervous system, making the werebeast stronger and violent, and driving the werebeast to kill. No known cure exists.

mortem provocatio A fight to the death.

North American *Were* **Council** The governing body of *weres* in North America, led by a president and several council members.

potestatem bonum "The power of good." That which encloses the earth and keeps demons from remaining among the living.

Purebloods (aka *pures***)** Werebeasts from generations of *were*-only family members. Considered royalty among werebeasts, they carry the responsibilities of their species. The mating between two purebloods is the only way to guarantee the conception of a *were* child.

rogue witch a witch without a coven. Must be accounted for as rogue witches tend to go one of two ways without a coven: dark or insane.

shape-shifter Evil, immortal creatures who can take any form. They are born witches, then spend years seeking innocents to sacrifice to a dark deity. When the deity deems the offerings sufficient, the witch casts a baneful spell to surrender his or her magic and humanity in exchange for immortality and the power of hell at their fingertips. Shape-shifters can command any form and are the deadliest and strongest of all mystical creatures.

shift Celia's ability to break down her body into minute particles. Her gift allows her to travel beneath and across soil, concrete, and rock. Celia can also *shift* a limited number of beings. Disadvantages include not being able to breathe or see until she surfaces.

Skinwalkers Creatures spoken of in whispers and believed to be *weres* damned to hell for turning on their kind. A humanoid combination of animal and man that reeks of death, a *skinwalker* can manipulate the elements and subterranean arachnids. Considered impossible to kill.

solis natus magicae The proper term for sunlight born of magic, created by a wielder of spells. Considered "pure" light. Capable of destroying non-master vampires and demons. In large quantities may also kill shape-shifters. Renders the wielder helpless once fired.

Superior Witch A witch of tremendous power and magic who assumes a leadership role among the coven. Wears a talisman around her neck or carries staff with a precious stone at its center to help amplify her magic.

Surface Celia's ability to reemerge from a shift.

susceptor animae A being capable of taking one's soul, such as a vampire.

Trudhilde Radinka (aka *Destiny*) A female born once every century from the union of two witches who possesses rare talents and the aptitude to predict the future. Considered among the elite of the mystical world.

turn To transform a human into a werebeast or vampire. Werebeasts *turn* by piercing the heart of a human with their fangs and transferring a part of their essence. Vampires pierce through the skull and into the brain to transfer a taste of their magic. Werebeasts risk their lives during the *turning* process, as they are gifting a part of their souls. Should the transfer fail, both the werebeast and human die. Vampires risk nothing since they're not losing their souls, but rather taking another's and releasing it from the human's body.

vampire A being who consumes the blood of mortals to survive. Beautiful and alluring, vampires will never appear to age past thirty years. Vampires are immune to sunlight unless it is created by magic. They are also immune to objects of faith such as crucifixes. Vampires may be killed by the destruction of their hearts, decapitation, or fire. Master vampires or vampires several centuries old must have both their hearts and heads removed or their bodies completely destroyed.

vampire clans Families of vampires led by master vampires. Masters can control, communicate, and punish their keep through mental telepathy.

velum A veil conjured by magic.

virtutem lucis "The power of light." The goodness found within each mortal. That which combats the darkness.

Warrior A werebeast possessing profound skill or fighting ability. Only the elite among *weres* are granted the title of Warrior. Warriors are duty-bound to protect their Leaders and their Leaders' mates at all costs.

werebeast A supernatural predator with the ability to *change* from human to beast. Werebeasts are considered the Guardians of the Earth against mystical evil. Werebeasts will achieve their first *change* within six months to a year following birth. The younger they are when they first *change,* the more powerful they will be. Werebeasts also possess the ability to heal their wounds. They can live until the first full moon following their one hundredth birthday. Werebeasts may be killed by destruction of their hearts, decapitation, or if their bodies are completely destroyed. The only time a *were* can partially *change* is when he or she attempts to *turn* a human. A *turned* human will achieve his or her first *change* by the next full moon.

witch A being born with the power to wield magic. They worship the earth and nature. Pure witches will not take part in blood sacrifices. They cultivate the land to grow plants for their potions and use staffs and talismans to amplify their magic. To cross a witch is to feel the collective wrath of her coven.

witch fire Orange flames encased by magic, used to assassinate an enemy. Witch fire explodes like multiple grenades when the intended victim nears the spell. Flames will continue to burn until the target has been eliminated.

zombie Typically human bodies raised from the dead by a necromancer witch. It's illegal to raise or keep a zombie and is among the deadliest sins in the supernatural world. Their diet consists of other dead things such as roadkill and decaying animals.

Photo by Kate Gledhill of Kate Gledhill Photography

Cecy Robson (also writing as Rosalina San Tiago for the app Hooked) is an author of contemporary romance, young adult adventure, and award-winning urban fantasy. A double RITA® 2016 finalist for Once Pure and Once Kissed, and a published author of more than twenty novels, you can typically find Cecy on her laptop writing her stories or stumbling blindly in search of caffeine.

www.cecyrobson.com

Facebook.com/Cecy.Robson.Author

instagram.com/cecyrobsonauthor

twitter.com/cecyrobson

www.goodreads.com/goodreadscomCecyRobsonAuthor

For exclusive information and more, join my Newsletter!

http://eepurl.com/4ASmj